The Mystery
of the Plant That
Ate Dirty Socks

NANCY MCARTHUR says, "I start my books with lots of ideas, but many more unfold as I write, so sometimes I am surprised by what happens." She has written six other books about Michael and Norman and their amazing plants and lives in Berea, Ohio, a suburb of Cleveland.

The Mystery of the Plant That Ate Dirty Socks

Nancy McArthur

AN AVON CAMELOT BOOK

THE MYSTERY OF THE PLANT THAT ATE DIRTY SOCKS is an original publication of Avon Books. This work has never before appeared in book form.

AVON BOOKS
A division of
The Hearst Corporation
1350 Avenue of the Americas
New York, New York 10019

Copyright © 1996 by Nancy McArthur
Published by arrangement with the author
Library of Congress Catalog Card Number: 95-96106
ISBN: 0-380-78318-5
RL: 4.9

First Avon Camelot Printing: July 1996

CAMELOT TRADEMARK REG. U.S. PAT. OFF. AND IN OTHER COUNTRIES, MARCA REGIS-TRADA, HECHO EN U.S.A.

Printed in the U.S.A.

OPM   10 9 8 7 6 5 4 3 2 1

To an author who gave me and my sister so much reading fun when we were children: Mildred Wirt Benson, who, early in her long and prolific career, wrote the original versions of twenty-three of the Nancy Drew books under the Carolyn Keene pseudonym.

Thanks to: Sherlock Holmes and Sir Arthur Conan Doyle for the dog clue; Edgar Allan Poe for the purloined letter clue; Nick Stiner-Riley; Emma Stiner-Riley; Margaret Stiner; Susan McArthur; Barbara and John McArthur and their dog, Goldie; Susan Cohen; Kate Bryant; Karen Kotrba; Jan C. Kempthorne-Snow; Mary C. Ryan; the real Pat Jenkins; Virginia Barenok; Gary Stocals.

Chapter 1

A crash of thunder rattled the window panes. Rain drummed on the roof. Outside in the dark, trees creaked in the wind. In the small pool of light from his bedside lamp, Michael was propped up on his pillow reading *The Curse of the Evil Ooze*.

"The giant blob of slime oozed slowly toward me," he read silently, "green and bubbling with a horrible smell. I was trapped between two huge fallen stone blocks in the pyramid passageway. I struggled to free myself—but all I could move was my fingers!"

Next to Michael's bed stood his six-foot-tall dirty-sock-eating pet plant, Stanley. Next to the other bed stood Fluffy, his younger brother's clean-sock-eating plant. Norman, the neatness nut and expert pest, was in the bathroom getting ready for bed. Michael was enjoying reading his book without Norman bothering him.

Stanley tapped him on the shoulder with a vine and tried to grab the book with another.

"Don't bother me right now," Michael told his plant in the tone he usually used only on Norman. "I want to read a couple more chapters."

He read on: "The ooze crept closer and closer, getting higher and higher. The smell was so bad I thought I was going to pass out. Closer and closer it came, melting small stones in its path. It was just three inches from my big toe, then two inches, then only one inch, when suddenly . . ."

As Michael started to turn the page, the light went out.

"Oh, man!" he groaned. "Right at the best part!"

For a moment, he thought Stanley might have turned off the lamp to get his attention. Or maybe the bulb burned out. But the light in the hall was out, too. This was total darkness.

He heard Dad exclaim from the living room down the hall, "Of all the dumb times for a power failure! Right in the middle of a play-off game! The street lights are out. It must be the whole neighborhood."

Mom yelled from the living room, "Michael, where did you put the flashlight?"

"I think in here someplace," he called. "I'll look for it!" He put the book aside and slid off the bed. "Oops!" He tripped over one of Stanley's vines and went sprawling on the rug. Although he couldn't see anything, he could smell the dirty socks he had put there for Stanley's late-night dinner. Fortunately, they did not smell anywhere near as bad as the evil ooze.

Mom called, "I'll get the candles from the dining room table. Everybody keep calm. The power company usually gets the electricity back on pretty soon." Michael heard the clunk of something falling over and a crash of breaking glass.

"Oops," said Mom. "I think I just broke the green lamp. Who put that table there?"

"You did," said Dad, "when you rearranged the living room furniture yesterday. Stay put. I'll get the candles. Ooof!"

"What happened?" asked Mom.

Dad replied, "I'm okay. I just fell over the couch."

Mom called, "Michael! Hurry up and find that flashlight!"

"I'm trying!" he reported.

"Norman?" called Mom. "Help your brother look!"

Norman's muffled voice yelled, "I can't find the door to get out of the bathroom! I thought I was opening the door, but it was the closet. A bunch of towels and rolls of toilet paper fell out all over. They're tripping me!"

"Don't move," Mom called. "I'm coming to get you!" Her voice sounded closer. She was feeling her way along the hall.

Michael fumbled around and found the knob on the drawer on his side of the table between his and Norman's beds. He took the drawer out and put it beside him on his bed to feel around inside it for the flashlight. He heard leaves rustling and skateboard wheels rolling. Both plants' large pots were fastened to skateboards to make them easier to move. They had learned to use their vines to grab onto furniture and pull themselves around.

"Stanley, stop," warned Michael. "Stay where you are." But the wheels kept rolling. Stanley usually did what Michael asked him to, so this must be Fluffy. He reached out and found Stanley near his regular spot. He reached for where he thought Fluffy might be, but he grasped only air.

4

"Fluffy, stop," he ordered. But Fluffy kept going. Michael gave up. Sometimes Fluffy panicked when he was separated from Norman at night. Once, when Norman was sleeping over at his best friend Bob's, Fluffy had escaped from the house trying to find him. First he nearly got taken by the trash truck. Then he rolled downhill and they had to chase him for blocks.

Now Michael heard Fluffy bumping into walls and furniture. He didn't seem to be getting out of the room.

Michael felt his way back to the drawer on the bed. Like all his drawers, it was a snarled-up mess. Michael had been the world's messiest kid, but he had changed his ways. It was part of the deal with Dad and Mom: neatness in exchange for the boys keeping their plants. Now he had to put things away instead of strewing them all over. Often he couldn't remember what he had put where. He touched every object in the drawer, but the flashlight wasn't there. Where else could he have put it?

"Stanley, do you know where I put the flashlight?" he asked. Leaves rustled. A vine grabbed him by the arm and yanked him off the bed. The drawer on his lap went flying. He heard small objects hitting the rug. Stanley dragged himself and Michael to Michael's bureau. The plant pulled open a drawer with such force that it fell out, dumping its contents. Michael dropped to his knees and began feeling around. Just as his fingers found the flashlight, from the hall came a bloodcurdling scream.

Chapter 2

Michael knew the scream had to be from Mom. It sounded like she had met the evil ooze. With trembling fingers, he switched on the flashlight. Its eerie glow threw tall shadows on the hallway wall. Mom was locked in what looked like mortal combat—with Fluffy.

When she saw what she was wrestling with, she let go and put her hand over her heart. Dad ran toward her.

Norman was yowling, "What happened? What happened?"

"It's okay," Mom assured him through the door.

"What happened?" asked Dad, putting an arm around her.

"Something big ran right into me. I had no

idea it was Fluffy. For a minute there, I felt like I was starring in a horror movie. What's this plant doing out in the hall?"

"Trying to get to Norman," said Michael. Dad took the flashlight and turned the bathroom doorknob.

"It's locked," he said. "Norman, unlock the door."

"I told you," replied Norman. "I can't *find* the door."

Dad aimed the light down. "Can you see a line of light on the floor? That's where the door is." They saw the knob turn, but the door didn't open.

Norman reported, "I can't see to work the lock. I'm flipping it back and forth, but it's not opening. It's stuck—or broke."

Mom sighed. "Maybe we could take the hinges apart and take the door off." Dad inspected the thick round metal pins that held the hinges together.

"They've been painted over a lot," he said, "so this'll take quite a while."

"Get me out of here!" wailed Norman. "I don't want to sleep all night in the bathroom all by myself in the dark! I want to sleep in my own bed next to Fluffy!" His plant grabbed the doorknob with a vine and tried to turn it.

8

"He can't stay locked in there all night," said Michael, "because I have to go to the bathroom right now."

Dad said, "A light through the window might work. I'll go outside and shine the flashlight in so Norman can see how to unlock the door. If that doesn't work, I'll climb in the window and try to remove the lock. Does anybody know where my battery-powered screwdriver is?"

"In the kitchen silverware drawer," said Mom. "It's still pouring out. Take an umbrella."

"Not in a lightning storm," said Dad. "Nobody should go out in this. I'll make a dash for it."

Mom and Michael sat on the floor beside the bathroom door. Michael patted Fluffy's leaves to calm him down. That always worked with Stanley. Dad went away with the flashlight, leaving them in the dark. They heard him thrashing around in the closet by the front door, looking for his raincoat.

Mom explained to Norman what Dad was going to do. While they waited, she started singing "Oh Susanna," one of Norman's favorites. Norman joined in on his side of the door. Michael knew Fluffy was waving his vines in time to the music because the plant kept hitting him on the head. Thunder boomed, making it hard to hear one another.

Meanwhile, Dad opened the back door and plunged out into the storm. A jagged line of lightning split the sky far in the distance. For a moment, it made the night as bright as day. There was so much water in the backyard, it looked like a lake.

Dad rapped on the bathroom window and shouted instructions to Norman, then aimed the flashlight at the lock. Now that Norman could see what he was doing, he tried turning it every which way. It still wouldn't open.

"I'm coming in," said Dad. He took the storm window off, and Norman opened the inside window. Dad handed Norman the flashlight and crawled in, almost falling on his head.

"I'm in," he yelled to Mom and Michael. Instead of hearing the whirr of the power screwdriver, they heard Dad say, "Uh-oh!"

"What's wrong?" asked Mom.

"My power screwdriver's dead. The last person who used it didn't put it back on the recharger—whoever that was."

"I guess that was me," admitted Mom. "Can't you just use it like a non-electric screwdriver?"

"It's going to take longer," replied Dad.

Michael sighed. "First we had only one person stuck in the bathroom. Now we've got two."

After a while, Mom called to Dad, "How long do you think this is going to take?" There was no answer. Mom pounded on the door. "Hey! Are you all right in there?" No one answered. The only sounds were another boom of thunder and the rain beating on the roof.

The back door slammed. Soon a dim light appeared at the end of the hall, followed by Dad. Because he was behind the flashlight, they could not see him very well. But they could hear him. His sneakers went *squish, squish, squish*. Behind him walked Norman, who did not squish because he was barefoot.

Dad said, "The wind's blowing so hard it's raining sideways out there." Mom took the flashlight and turned it on him. He looked as if he had been swimming with all his clothes on. His raincoat was soaked through. His wet hair was plastered flat down over his forehead.

"You look like a drowned rat," said Mom.

"Gee, thanks," replied Dad. "That really cheers me up."

"You didn't wear a hat?" she wondered.

"I did. My fishing hat. The wind took it. I loved that hat, and it's probably halfway to

11

Elmville by now. What I needed out there was scuba gear!"

Mom said, "Maybe we'll find your hat in the morning. It could have stayed in the neighborhood. Why didn't you take the lock off?"

"Because I realized it has some more screws on this side of the door."

Michael held the flashlight for Dad while he worked on the lock.

"If anybody needs to go to the bathroom before I get the door open," Dad said, "I left the window open."

"You're joking," said Mom.

"No, I didn't stop to close it. We just made a dash for the back door."

"But it must be raining in," she said. "We'll have water running out from under the door any minute."

Norman, who enjoyed thinking up possible worst things that could happen, asked, "But what if a burglar climbs in the window while it's open?"

Dad assured him, "Any burglar dumb enough to be out in a storm like this would drown before he got in."

Dad removed the last screw and pulled the lock out. The door swung open. Michael took the flashlight in and closed the door.

"Close the window!" called Mom. Michael kicked aside fallen towels and toilet paper rolls to make a path to the window, toilet, and sink. When he started to brush his teeth, he noticed squiggles of green toothpaste in the sink. Norman must have been trying to squeeze it on his brush in the dark and missed.

Things finally got settled down. Mom found the matches to light the candles and gave the flashlight to the boys. Michael just wanted to crawl into bed, but first he had to crawl around on the floor and pick up all the stuff Stanley had dumped from drawers. In the past, the plants had eaten things that made them sick, so he had to make sure nothing small enough to eat was left near them on the floor except their socks dinner.

Norman, snuggled in his bed, watched Michael crawl around and refused to help. When Michael finished, he looked for *The Curse of the Evil Ooze*. Now that he had a light, he wanted to find out what happened next before he went to sleep.

He looked on his bed and under it. He ran his hand between the wall and the bed. He felt under his pillow and among the sheets and blanket. The book had vanished.

Chapter 3

Michael turned to the most likely suspect, the one that had been trying to grab the book earlier.

"Stanley," he asked, "did you hide my book? Point to where you put it." Stanley stood still, ignoring his question. Michael looked everywhere that the plant might have stashed the book—in drawers, behind the bedside table, behind the curtains, under the edges of the rug.

"It's the mystery of the missing book," said Norman. "Want me to get out my detective kit?"

"No," said Michael. "I don't think putting on your fake glasses disguise with the funny nose and moustache would solve this case."

He flashed the light around the room, wondering where to search next. If the book hadn't fallen under the bed or gotten tangled up in the covers, and if Stanley hadn't put it somewhere, then that left . . .

He aimed the flashlight at Norman's face. When he had brushed his teeth in the dark, he had missed his mouth. Smeared on his upper lip was a crooked little green toothpaste moustache. Michael decided not to tell him. Maybe the toothpaste would crumble off. Norman hated crumbs in bed. It would serve him right.

Michael exclaimed, "You hid my book, didn't you!"

"I did not!" replied Norman. "I didn't even see your dumb book!"

"Then maybe Fluffy picked it up. Get out of bed! I'm searching your side of the room."

"Stay on your own side," snarled Norman. "I don't want you messing up my side!"

"Aha! That means you *do* have something to hide. Move!"

"No!" insisted Norman. He pulled the covers over his head and held on tightly. Michael could not get through the top of this cocoon. He stuck his hand farther down under the covers and began tickling Norman's feet. Norman wriggled and scrunched up to avoid him. Michael kept tickling.

Fluffy wound vines around Michael's arms, trying to pull him away. Norman's shrieks brought Mom and Dad, carrying their candles.

They found the boys wrestling on Norman's bed, Fluffy trying to pull Michael off Norman, and Stanley trying to pull Fluffy off Michael. With so many vines involved, they were all in a terrible tangle.

"Stop it!" commanded Dad.

Michael said, "He hid my book! Or if he didn't, Fluffy took it. I was just trying to get it back!"

"I did not!" protested Norman. "And neither did Fluffy!"

Dad asked Michael, "What made you think Norman or Fluffy took it?"

"I looked everywhere I could have lost it or Stanley could have put it."

Dad advised, "You can't jump to wild conclusions and accuse people without proof. You have to use logical thinking."

"But I did," protested Michael.

"You were wrong," said Dad.

Mom asked, "Where did you have it last?"

"On my bed. I was reading it when the lights went out. Right at the best part! Kevin was trapped and the evil ooze was coming right at

16

him. It was only one inch from his big toe. I have to find out what happened!"

"Get in bed," said Dad. "The book has to be in this room somewhere. You'll find it in the morning. Don't worry. The hero always escapes somehow."

"But I want to know how right now," said Michael.

Mom tucked in his covers. "I don't want you to read scary stuff like that at bedtime," she said.

"But these are the best scary stories," protested Michael. "This is the twelfth one in that series I've read."

"Good," said Mom. "Then you'll be done with the series soon, and you can start on something more worthwhile."

Michael thought that now would not be a good time to mention that there were thirty-eight more he hadn't read yet. He gave Stanley a goodnight pat and drifted off to sleep, to the sound of rain beating on the roof.

Soon after everyone fell asleep, the rain slowed to a soft pattering. The plants began to stir, ready to eat.

Chapter 4

Stanley reached a vine across the floor and twined it around a dirty sock. He lifted it to one of the ice-cream-cone-shaped leaves the plants used for sucking in socks. *Schlurrrp!* The sock slowly disappeared. After a while, he burped. Then he fed himself another sock. Fluffy began to do the same with his dinner of clean socks. *Schlurrrp! Burrrrpp! Schlurrp! Burrrp!* Each of Fluffy's burps was also followed by a noise that sounded like "Ex," because Norman had tried to teach his plant to say "Excuse me."

Early in the morning, Norman was the first one up, as usual. Mom always said he was a human alarm clock. This came in handy today

18

because all their clocks were electric and the power was still off.

To Michael, Norman was worse than a real alarm clock. A clock just buzzed at the set time until you turned it off. But Norman could not be turned off. He sang loudly and off-key if he was in the mood for music. He jumped on beds or made other noises to pester Michael into getting up. Sometimes he worked on teaching Fluffy new tricks and bothered Michael until he got up to teach Stanley, too, before Dad and Mom awakened.

The daylight made searching for the book easier. Michael looked all over. He still couldn't find it.

Before breakfast, they all went out to see what damage the storm had done. Large tree limbs had fallen on lawns and sidewalks. An enormous tree lay across one yard with its huge clump of roots and soil tipped up out of the ground. It had just missed hitting the nearby house. Little bunches of tree leaves torn off by the winds littered every yard. At the far end of the street, a power company crew with a big yellow truck was working on getting the electricity back on. Many neighbors were out looking around and talking.

"Did your basement flood?" Dad asked the Wards, their older next-door neighbors.

"We've got a foot of water down there," replied Mr. Ward. "The electric pump that goes on when heavy rain starts seeping in stopped when the power went off."

"That's awful," said Mom.

"We've been through this before," said Mrs. Ward. "So we keep everything high up on shelves. You're so lucky that your basement never floods. Did you have any problems?"

"Not really," Mom said. "The lock on the bathroom door got stuck with Norman in there, and it took us a while to find the only flashlight in the house. It made me realize that we're not well-prepared for emergencies."

Mr. Ward said, "I was going to come over this evening to tell you we're leaving for Arizona the day after tomorrow. We'll be gone two months. Since we both retired, we don't have to rush back in two weeks like last year. The dry weather there made my arthritis feel so much better, we decided to stay longer this year."

Mrs. Ward added, "And we won't have to ask you to keep checking on our house this time. We've rented it to a nice young man we met in Arizona last year. He's coming here to start a business and wanted to rent a place while he looks for a house to buy. It'll be much better than having our house empty so long."

Dad asked, "What kind of business is he in?"

"Sales," said Mr. Ward. "His name's Aldrich. He'll be arriving the day after we leave. We'd appreciate it if we could tell him he can call on you if he has any questions."

"Sure," said Dad. "I hope you have a wonderful time in Arizona."

Norman was getting bored listening to all this. So he was glad to see his favorite neighbor, Mrs. Smith, who lived four houses down, coming along the sidewalk with her small brown dog, Margo, on a leash. Mrs. Smith was Norman's favorite, because she thought anything he did was wonderful. The rest of the family liked her a lot, too, because she was such a good neighbor.

"What a mess!" she said. "I'm sorry to see that great old tree destroyed. But we're lucky the damage wasn't any worse." Margo wagged her tail at Norman. He squatted down to pat her.

Someone at the end of the street yelled, "The power's back on!"

Mom told Mrs. Smith, "Come in and have breakfast with us. We haven't had a chance to

21

talk for a while. Isn't your California trip coming up soon?"

"Yes. A three-week trip takes a lot of getting ready, but I know I'm going to have fun. My sister and I are going to stay at a wonderful hotel and go to the meeting of the National African Violet Society."

As Mom and Dad put food on the table, Mrs. Smith asked Michael, "Would you like a plant-sitting job while I'm away? You took such good care of my African violets the last time."

"Okay," said Michael gladly. "When do you want to bring them over?"

Mom suggested, "Maybe we should leave them at your house. Even though they're small, forty African violets take up a lot of space."

"I have more now," said Mrs. Smith, chuckling.

Dad asked, "Are you still president of the local African violet club?"

"Yes, and I really enjoy it."

Norman said, "Did you get to be president 'cause you have the most violets?"

"No, you don't have to have a lot to join or be president. You just have to be interested. You know, there are clubs for lots of other kinds of plants—roses, orchids, dahlias—just to name a few. The other day I saw a bumper

22

sticker that said 'Gourd Power.' It was from a gourd group. Maybe you and Michael could start your own club for your kind of plants."

"It'd be a very small club," remarked Mom. "The boys have the only ones we know of except for some grown from their seeds that we gave to our botanist friend, Susan Sparks, for experiments—and a couple that we sold to a botanical garden."

Mrs. Smith said, "You can have a club with only two people if you want to." Michael made a face at the thought of being in a club with Norman. "Or," she told Norman, "you can start some other kind of club. What else are you interested in?"

Norman thought a moment. "Everything," he replied.

"That's good," she said. "But to start a club, you might want to narrow that down a little. Unless you want to call it The Everything Club."

As they ate, Margo rubbed against Norman's leg.

"Does Margo like hotels?" he asked.

"Hotels don't allow dogs. I have to put her in the kennel, even though she doesn't like it."

"What's the kennel?"

"It's like a hotel for pets. The vet I take

23

Margo to for her checkups runs one in the same building with his animal hospital."

"Does she get her own room there?" asked Norman.

"No, a cage. But the dogs are let out to run in a fenced-in area on a regular schedule."

"It sounds like a pet jail," said Michael.

Mrs. Smith replied, "The kennel takes very good care of animals. But Margo was really glad to get home the one time I had to leave her there. It's expensive, but I don't have any other choice."

Margo rolled over for Norman to rub her tummy. He wondered if anybody at the kennel would rub her tummy every time she wanted.

He said, "Margo can come stay here. Can't she, Mom? Can't she, Dad? I'll take good care of her."

Mrs. Smith smiled and shook her head. "A dog is a big responsibility," she said. "When you're a little older, you can do it."

"I can do it now!" said Norman. "I always take good care of Fluffy."

"That's true," she agreed. "But a dog is more work than a plant."

Mom said to Dad, "What do you think?"

He replied, "It might be nice to have a dog for a little while."

"Let me do it," pleaded Norman. "Please? Please? Please?"

Dad told Mom, "It's up to you."

"All right," she decided.

"Yes!" Norman shouted.

Chapter 5

After Mrs. Smith and Margo left, Michael complained, "I still can't find my book."

Mom suggested, "Retrace your steps. You'll probably discover it's right where you put it."

"But I didn't put it anywhere!"

Dad said from behind the newspaper, "Maybe it's hidden right under your nose. Like that famous detective story by Edgar Allan Poe, 'The Purloined Letter.' "

"What's *purloined*?" asked Norman.

"Stolen," said Dad.

"Then why didn't he call it the stolen letter?" asked Michael.

Dad replied, "Maybe he just liked 'purloined' better. It's an old-fashioned word now, but not when he was writing. Anyway, in the story, an important letter was stolen by a blackmailer. He hid it where people could see it but didn't notice it. He'd turned it inside out and put it with some other papers."

"Hiding something in plain sight is pretty clever," said Mom.

"Edgar Allan Poe was brilliant," said Dad. "He invented the detective story. And he was excellent at horror stories, too."

"My book isn't hidden where I can see it," said Michael. "I looked everywhere."

"Use your logical thinking ability," advised Dad. "You know what your mother always says whenever something weird happens: there must be a logical explanation."

"But I can't think of a logical explanation."

"I can," boasted Norman. "Your book grew wings and flew away. Ha! Ha!"

Michael flicked some soggy cereal flakes at him and missed.

"Pick that up!" snapped Mom. "Right now!"

Dad continued, "Try thinking about clues and make deductions. Like Sherlock Holmes. Or the Hardy boys."

Norman added, "Like Encyclopedia Brown."

Mom said, "Like Nancy Drew. She was my favorite when I was a kid."

Michael told Dad, "I don't have any clues to think about."

Dad replied, "We could practice on a real mystery. Let's see what's in the paper. Here's a jewel theft—a house was broken into and a valuable necklace was stolen. Wait, here's a better one. You'll like this. It's about a plant."

He read aloud: " 'A rare Chinese shrub was stolen right out of a local family's backyard, police said yesterday. Olaf and Marie Sorensen, 647 Oak Street, returned from a weekend trip Sunday night and found a large hole where the plant had been.'

" 'I'm very upset about this,' said Sorensen. 'That plant was important to me. My grandfather brought it back from China many years ago, and we've shared cuttings in our family. If someone wanted one of these, I would have been glad to give him a cutting to root. If my shrub isn't returned, I'll have to get a cutting myself from one of my brothers and start over.'

" 'Police said the Sorensen family is offering a fifty-dollar reward. Anyone who has any information should call the police department.' "

Norman said excitedly, "We can use our logical thinking and find the shrub and get the reward!" He paused to think a moment and asked, "What's a shrub?"

"A bush," said Dad.

Norman suggested, "Let's go over to Oak Street and look for clues!"

"Hold it!" said Dad. "This mystery is just for thinking practice, not for actually running around detecting."

"We could just be on the lookout for it," said Norman. "In case we see it by accident. Then we could get the reward!"

"No shrub hunting," said Dad. "Just mental exercise. Pretend you're detectives on the case. Think of questions."

"Like what?" asked Michael.

"Like why would anybody steal the shrub?"

Norman said, "They wanted one for their yard, and they're too cheap to buy one."

"Or," said Michael, "they're going to sell it to someone who'll pay a lot of money for it."

"For a shrub?" asked Mom.

"If there aren't very many of them," said Michael, "maybe it's worth a lot of money."

Mom said, "Cutting a branch and growing roots on it would probably take several years to turn into a good-sized shrub. Maybe someone wanted a big one right now."

Michael said, "The crook must be somebody who knows a lot about plants."

"See?" said Dad. "Isn't this interesting? You're using your logical thinking skills."

Michael said, "But I still don't know where my book is."

Norman said, "Let's call the police and tell them what we thought of."

"No," said Dad.

"But the newspaper says to call if we have any information," Norman pointed out.

"We don't have any information," said Dad.

"But what if I accidentally see the shrub somewhere even though I'm not looking?"

"Tell your mother or me, and we'll call the police."

"Then will you get the reward instead of me?"

"No," said Dad. "We have to get going. We've spent so much time talking, now we're running late."

In the flurry to get ready for school, Michael couldn't find his notes for his school project. Norman insisted he needed a shirt that wasn't in his drawer. They both called for Mom to help them.

"Hold on!" she exclaimed. "I can't be in two places at once."

Norman suggested helpfully, "You could get cloned. Then there would be two of you."

"One of me is enough," said Mom. She found Michael's notes under a magazine in the living room. Norman's shirt was in the laundry basket, still unwashed, so he had to wear another one.

As the boys went out the door, Norman told Michael, "I bet I accidentally see that shrub before you do. Then I'll get the reward."

"Dream on," replied Michael.

After the boys left, Dad said, "What have I started? They're probably going to be on shrub patrol all over town."

"Don't worry," said Mom. "They don't know how to find it."

"How can you be sure?" asked Dad.

"Because they don't have a clue about what it looks like. The article didn't say."

Dad gave her a hug. "Good logical thinking," he said with a grin.

"Just call me Sherlock," she said, laughing.

Chapter 6

When Michael got to school, he asked his friend Chad Palmer, "Have you read *The Curse of the Evil Ooze?*"

"Probably," replied Chad. "I've read so many of that series, I can't exactly remember."

"Do you remember the part where Kevin gets trapped by the rocks in the pyramid and the evil ooze is almost up to his big toe?"

"No, what happened?"

When Michael started explaining about his lost book, Pat Jenkins came across the room to stick her nose into their conversation. Michael thought she had radar ears because she was good at overhearing scraps of what people were saying, even from far off.

"You lost something?" she asked.

32

"Yeah," said Michael, not wanting to tell her all the details.

"I know how to find lost things," she said. "You try to think like whatever it was you lost."

"Huh?" replied Michael.

"Like when I lost my lunch," continued Pat. "I mean my lunch box. I went back to where I remembered I had it last. Then I asked myself, 'If I were my lunch box, where would I be?' Then I pictured the places I could possibly be and looked in those places and there it was."

Their teacher, Mrs. Black, told them to take their seats and be quiet, so Michael and Chad did not find out where Pat had found her lunch box. But as Mrs. Black talked about what they were going to do today, Michael could not help picturing Pat Jenkins as a lunch box, with her face on the side, little arms and legs sticking out, and very big ears.

As they settled down to some quiet work, from the music room next door floated ear-splitting noises—*squeak, tootle, squeal, squonk.* Another batch of beginners was starting to learn to blow notes on flutophones. Michael wondered how the music teacher could stand it. Mrs. Black closed their door.

* * *

A police officer was spending the week at Edison Elementary to visit classrooms and talk to kids about how to stay out of trouble. He had told everybody to call him Officer Tim and to feel free to ask him about anything.

So when Norman saw him in the hall, he asked, "What does that purloined shrub look like? The one with the reward?"

"Purloined?" said Officer Tim, looking surprised.

"That means swiped," said Norman.

"I know," replied Officer Tim. "But how did you know? You look a little young to be reading that Edgar Allan Poe story."

"My dad told me about it."

"Why do you want to know about the shrub?"

"Just in case I accidentally see it someplace. Then I could call the police."

"It looks like an ordinary bush," said Officer Tim. "You'd have to be a plant expert or have a leaf to compare to identify it. But it's probably not still in this town. Stolen rare plants are usually sold to buyers far away who are willing to pay high prices. Some don't know the plants are stolen, or don't ask where they came from."

Norman asked, "Crooks purloin plants to sell?"

"Yes. Hard-to-get kinds—and endangered

species—or rare ones from other countries. There are laws against bringing certain plants into this country or taking them out. Some states have laws like that, too. Sometimes tourists try to sneak plants in, but smugglers do a big business secretly carrying illegal things from one country to another."

"Like what?" asked Norman.

"Like rare orchids. They steal them right out of the rainforests. A smuggler who brings back a suitcase full can sell them for a thousand dollars apiece."

"They can get rich," remarked Norman.

Officer Tim said, "They can also get caught. And pay big fines and go to prison."

"It serves them right," said Norman. "Stealing is wrong."

Officer Tim replied, "You're so right." He looked at Norman as if trying to recall where he had seen him before. "You look familiar," he said. "What's your name? Where do you live?"

Norman told him.

"Now I remember. You're the family with those two big weird plants—the ones on skateboards that rolled away a couple of times and had you chasing them all over town. We haven't had any calls from your family about escaped plants for a long time. You must have taken our advice about not taking them out of the house."

But they *had* taken Stanley and Fluffy to school for Pet Plant Day (a big uproar) and to a natural history museum where Fluffy tangled with a robot planteater dinosaur (an even bigger uproar). And Stanley had gone up on a space shuttle flight as a plant experiment to pick up trash and eat the astronauts' dirty socks (an uproar in orbit).

Norman replied truthfully, "We don't take them out very often. Just mostly in the backyard to get some sun."

"If they're rare," advised Officer Tim with a smile, "you better keep a close watch on them—in case the plant purloiners are still in town. But that shrub was probably what they came for, and they're long gone by now. People like that keep moving."

The rest of the day, at recess, at lunch, in gym, and every other chance Michael got, he kept trying to find someone who had read *The Curse of the Evil Ooze*—anyone who could recall how Kevin's big toe (and the rest of Kevin) had been saved from the killer goo. Just about everyone he asked had read some of the series. Kids were always boasting about how many they had read, but today no one he talked to recalled that particular escape.

Jason Greensmith said, "I read twelve. I'm on my thirteenth now—*The Revenge of the Werewolf Piano Teacher*. When I get done, want to trade?"

"My book is lost," said Michael, who did not want to trade with Jason. In the past, he had gotten the short end of some of their deals.

Jason said, "When you find it, let me know."

Chad boasted, "I read fifteen."

Pat Jenkins said, "I don't read scary stories. I like books about real things. That's more interesting."

"These stories are fun to read," Brad Chan told her. "I'm on my eighteenth."

But Kimberly Offenberg put an end to the bragging. "I've read thirty-nine," she said. "I have almost all of them."

Michael said, "Can I borrow *The Curse of the Evil Ooze?*"

"That's one I haven't got yet," said Kim.

Chapter 7

After school, Michael rode his bike to the public library to borrow a copy of the missing book. On the rack where the series was kept, there were only five, all ones he had read. He used the computer to request the book so he would get a phone call when it was his turn on the waiting list.

At home, after he had a snack and watered Stanley, he decided to retrace his steps, as Mom had suggested. He repeated every move he recalled making after the lights went out. He even closed his eyes to pretend he was in the dark. But he kept bumping into things and gave up.

He pulled the bedspread and sheets off his bed, shook them out, and dropped them on the floor. He took the pillow out of its case. Finally, he dragged the mattress off and pulled the bed away from the wall. No book.

Next he decided to try the Pat Jenkins method. He thought it was silly, but he couldn't think of anything else to do. He sat on the mattress in the middle of the floor and said aloud, "If I were my book, where would I be?"

Norman, who had overhead him, bounded into the room.

"I know where you'd be," he said. "On a bookshelf!" He looked around. "You wrecked the room!" he complained. "And your mattress is sticking over on my side!"

"Only a little bit," said Michael. Norman began jumping on the mattress. "Get off my mattress!" snarled Michael.

Norman replied, "The part I'm jumping on is on my side of the room!" He kept bouncing. Michael tackled him.

"Now you're on my side," he said. "Get off!"

Norman did not budge. Michael grabbed his ankles and pulled, but Norman clutched the edge of the mattress with both hands. Michael gave up.

Norman asked, "Aren't you going to look on your bookshelf?"

"No." Even though he wanted to find his

book, he did not want Norman to out-deduce him and be right. If he did, he would never stop bragging.

"You should look there. Maybe it's like the purloined letter."

"I didn't have it anywhere near the bookshelf."

Norman crawled over to Michael's bureau and stood up to look at the shelf above it. He took the books out, one by one. The missing one wasn't there. Then Norman went through his own bookshelf. It wasn't there, either.

When Dad got home from work, he asked Michael, "Did you find your book?"

"Nope. I looked everywhere." Dad sat down on Norman's bed and looked around the room.

"Well, if it's not anywhere on the floor or on any of the furniture, that reminds me of a famous quote from Sherlock Holmes—'When you have eliminated the impossible, whatever remains, however improbable, must be the truth.'"

"I don't get it," said Michael.

"You tried all the likely places," said Dad. "Let's try some unlikely places. How about the walls?"

"But that's impossible. There's nothing there except the mirror and a few pictures."

"Let's look behind them," said Dad. Michael had read some Sherlock Holmes stories and was really impressed with his father's logical thinking. They looked behind the mirror and pictures. No book.

"I give up," said Michael. "What would Sherlock Holmes do now?" He flopped on his bed.

"Was the window open?" asked Dad. "Could the book have gotten out that way somehow?"

"No."

Dad remarked, "I guess even Sherlock would give up on this one."

Michael said, "Can I have an advance on my allowance? I want to buy another copy of *The Curse of the Evil Ooze* if the library doesn't come through soon."

"How about reading something better?" asked Dad. "Like *Treasure Island*."

"What's it about?"

"A boy who gets mixed up with pirates, buried treasure, a sea voyage, terrifying danger, adventure, suspense, close escapes."

"Sounds good," said Michael. "A little like the series I'm reading now."

"Believe me," said Dad, "it's better."

As Michael lay on his bed staring at the ceil-

41

ing, he noticed that the light fixture up there had a wide white glass shield that hung under the two bulbs to cut down on glare.

He ran over to the light switch by the door and flicked it on. Laughing, he pointed up. Against the glass was a shadow just the size of the missing book.

"Sherlock was right!" he said. "A book being on the ceiling is impossible, but there it is!" Dad climbed up on a chair and got the book down.

"Why didn't you see this before?" he asked.

"That light wasn't turned on when the power went out," Michael said. "After the power came back on, we didn't turn it on because it was daytime."

"Great deduction, son," said Dad. "You're an excellent logical thinker. But how did the book get way up there?"

Michael turned to his first suspect—Stanley—who had a long enough reach with his top vines to put something up that high.

He told the plant, "You were trying to get my attention last night, but I kept reading. Is that why you hid the book?" He gave Stanley an affectionate pat. "Next time I won't ignore you."

He leafed quickly through the pages to find

the place where he had left off. "Listen to this," he told Dad. "This is really cool!" He read aloud: " 'Closer and closer it came, melting little stones in its path. It was just three inches from my big toe, then two inches, then only one inch, when suddenly . . .' "

Michael eagerly turned the page. " 'Stop!' boomed a hoarse voice. A shadowy figure dressed like an ancient Egyptian loomed on the far side of the ooze. 'O, Great Ooze, dark avenger from the past,' the voice called. 'Stop! Leave this mortal to me! I have a much worse fate planned for him!' I looked down. The ooze had stopped at his command—one half inch from my big toe. To my amazement . . .' "

Michael heard leaves rustling and looked up. Dad was on the edge of Norman's bed, leaning forward to listen. Stanley and Fluffy were leaning forward, too.

He read on: " 'To my amazement, the ooze started to roll away, still bubbling and stinking. The smell was getting fainter. The shadowy figure came closer. I cringed in horror as I saw his face. It was my father the archeologist's trusted assistant, Igor. The master of the evil ooze had been in our midst all along!' "

Mom called, "Dinner, everybody!"

Norman was in the living room watching the local TV news. Mom called him again.

"I'm coming," he replied, but kept sitting there.

At the table Michael, with a fork in one hand and his book in the other, began reading aloud.

Mom said, "Not now. I don't want to hear about evil ooze or any other kind of ooze while I'm eating. Where did you find your book?" Michael explained. "Excellent logical thinking," she said. Michael read on silently.

"Norman, get in here," yelled Dad.

"In a minute."

"Now!" ordered Dad. The program was ending, so Norman turned off the TV and came to the kitchen.

"What was so interesting on TV?" asked Mom.

"I was waiting for them to show a picture of that bush," said Norman. "But they didn't."

Michael said, "I knew they wouldn't show it."

"Why not?" asked Norman.

"Because nobody can take a picture of a bush that isn't there."

Norman said, "But they showed something really cool! A chimpanzee at a zoo that paints pictures! They showed him finger painting. The

44

zoo sells his pictures for three hundred dollars."

Michael looked up. "Apiece?" he asked.

"Yep. And they put them in real frames. Just like a real artist."

Mom said, "For three hundred dollars, they ought to throw in the chimp as part of the deal."

Norman remarked, "We could get rich if we had a chimpanzee that finger painted."

Michael said, "I saw a zoo elephant on TV a long time ago that was painting pictures. It held a brush with its trunk. They sold those pictures for a lot of money, too." He went back to reading his book.

"Oh, cool!" he exclaimed.

"What happened?" asked Dad.

"Igor tripped on his ancient Egyptian sandals and fell in the ooze. He got melted."

"Serves him right," said Dad. "A trustworthy assistant ought to be worthy of being trusted."

After dinner, Michael sprawled on his bed and started reading silently. Stanley grabbed the book and waved it at him. Michael pried it from the plant's clutches.

"Why are you doing this?" he asked. Then he realized that Stanley had not tried to grab the

45

book earlier when Michael was reading aloud. As a matter of fact, both plants had looked as if they were really interested.

Fluffy liked to be sung to by Norman. Maybe Stanley wanted to be read to. Michael began again, out loud: "I wiggled free at last of the huge fallen stone blocks that had trapped me and ran down the passageway. Was this the way out? Or would it lead me deeper into the pyramid? Suddenly, the floor dropped from beneath my feet. I was falling . . ." Michael turned the page. Stanley rustled his leaves contentedly.

Chapter 8

Early the next morning, Michael heard Norman say, "Oops! Not there! Here! Yeah, that looks good!"

Michael rolled over in bed to see what his brother was up to now.

With one hand, Norman was holding down the corner of a big piece of paper on the floor. The paper had red squiggles on it. In his other hand was a large open jar of red poster paint. But the one who was holding the paint brush was Fluffy.

"What are you doing?" yelled Michael.

"Sssh!" said Norman. "Don't wake up Mom and Dad. This is a surprise."

Michael warned, "You can't turn Fluffy loose with a wet brush. He'll get paint all over."

"No, he won't," Norman assured him. "See? I put a big piece of plastic over the middle of the rug. If any paint gets on that, I can wipe it off."

Michael noticed that the brush Fluffy was waving around was very small, about a quarter of an inch wide. The plant could not make much of a mess with that. Michael was glad that at least Norman had not decided to have Fluffy spray paint with his Super Splasher Water Blaster.

"Why are you doing this?" asked Michael.

"Fluffy's going to be an artist like the chimpanzee and the elephant. I'm going to sell his pictures for three hundred dollars." He smirked and added, "Apiece."

He guided Fluffy's vine to dip the brush into the jar and then to make more squiggles on the paper.

"But he's not doing the painting," said Michael. "You're making his vine move."

Norman protested, "He's just learning. I'm teaching him."

"Fluffy's not an artist," said Michael. "And neither are you."

"Don't say that," said Norman, scowling. "You'll make Fluffy mad."

48

Michael added, "Nobody'll pay five cents for a fake picture painted by a fake plant artist!"

Fluffy reached over with the brush and painted a red line across Michael's right cheek, over his nose, and across his left cheek. Then, for good measure, he also painted Michael's left ear.

Norman did a little dance of glee. "See? Fluffy *is* a real artist!" he exclaimed. "He painted you all by himself!"

Michael felt his ear. His fingers came away red. He wiped them on his pajama sleeve.

"I'll get you for this," he yelled at his brother.

"I didn't do it," said Norman with a grin. "Fluffy did."

"You made him do it," said Michael.

"Did not!"

"Did too!"

The door opened. "What's going on?" asked Mom. As she stared at the red stripe on Michael, Norman shoved the painting under his bed and snatched the brush from Fluffy.

"Face painting?" she said. "Before breakfast? There must be a logical explanation, but I can't imagine what it is."

Michael said, "Norman and Fluffy are messing around with paint."

"Hand it over," Mom ordered. Norman gave her the brush and paint jar.

"At least you had enough sense to cover the rug," she said. "The only painting you're allowed to do is artwork on paper. Not on your brother. Got that?"

"Yep," said Norman, with his most winning smile. "Just on paper."

That afternoon, when Michael got home from school, he heard horrible noises coming from the kitchen—*squeal, screech, tootle, toot, squeak, squeal, squonk!*

He pushed open the kitchen door. Norman and his friend Bob were blowing into flutophones.

"Oh, no!" exclaimed Michael. "You're not going to play those things here!"

"Oh, yes," replied Norman. "We're practicing. The music teacher said we should practice fifteen minutes every day."

Bob added, "He said if we get good, we can play in the flutophone band concert." He blew into his flutophone and moved his fingers up and down on the holes. *Squeak, squeal, toot.*

"First we have to learn how to make the notes," he explained.

"Why don't you go practice at Bob's house?" Michael asked.

"We already tried that," said Bob. "My mom told us to come over here."

Mom came into the kitchen. "I have to get dinner started now. Go practice in the garage."

"It's too cold out," said Norman.

Mom said, "Then go in your room." Norman and Bob picked up their instruction books and went down the hall.

Mom told Michael, "Margo has come to stay. Mrs. Smith's leaving in the morning. She wants you to stop by after dinner to get your plantsitting instructions and Margo's doggie bed."

Dad came in the back door. He kissed Mom and asked, "What's new?"

From down the hall, Norman and Bob started up again: *squeak, squonk, squeal, tootle, screech.*

Dad said, "Holy cow! It sounds like the smoke detectors are playing a duet! What is that?"

"Norman and Bob are learning to play fluto-phones," replied Mom. "When I signed the permission slip, I had no idea it was going to sound this bad."

Somewhere among the awful noises, Michael

thought he heard a couple that might be actual musical notes, but he couldn't be sure.

Dad said, "There can't be many things that sound worse than a flutophone being played badly."

Michael said, "Two flutophones."

Margo, who had been snoozing in the boys' room, began to howl: "Ow-oooo-owl!"

"That's worse," said Mom. "Two flutophones and a dog." As she went down the hall to stop this weird concert, Margo passed her at a gallop. Then Mom was almost run down by Fluffy and Stanley. They were pulling themselves out of the boys' room as fast as their skateboard wheels could carry them.

Norman told her, "I think Fluffy and Stanley don't like our music."

Mom said, "I don't think Margo likes it either."

"But she was singing along with us," said Norman.

"That wasn't singing. Your sounds must be hurting her ears. Dogs have very sensitive hearing. Go practice in the bathroom. With the door closed. Sit in the bathtub. Close the shower curtains. Maybe that'll muffle the sound."

Mom brought Margo into the kitchen. The

plants joined them. With the bathroom and kitchen doors closed, the screeching and squonking now sounded far enough away that they weren't driven nuts.

Dad said, "I'm all in favor of music lessons, but why did the teacher assign our child an instrument that he's misusing to make some of the most nerve-shattering noises known to man?"

"And woman," added Mom.

Dad said, "Tomorrow I'm calling that music teacher and telling him Norman has a talent for playing the triangle."

"Great," said Mom, "but what makes you think he has triangle talent?"

"He can learn," replied Dad. "I'd rather listen to *ting-ting-ting* than squealing that sounds like a bunch of very annoyed pigs."

Mom said, "It sounds more like an explosion in a whistle factory. Do you think we could get Bob switched to triangle, too?"

Dad said, "Let's talk to his parents."

Chapter 9

But at dinner, Norman did not go for Dad's idea. "The triangles hardly get to do anything," he explained. "They have to wait and wait for the part when they get to go *ting*. Then they have to wait a long time again. And what if you miss the part where you're supposed to go *ting*? It's easy to get mixed up if you start thinking about something else while you're waiting. The flutophones don't have to wait. We'll get to play almost all the time, so you can't think about something else."

Mom said, "But with the triangle, you wouldn't have to practice much to learn how to go *ting* at the right times."

Norman thought that over. "Sometimes the

triangles go *ting-ting* or *ting-a-ling* or other stuff you have to practice. Not just *ting*. Besides, I like practicing with Bob. It's more fun than by myself. We're developing our musical talent. The teacher said our musical talent needs a lot of developing."

Later Dad told Mom, "This is only the first day. Maybe the novelty will wear off. Or maybe he and Bob will actually learn to play music on those things."

"In the meantime," said Mom, "I'm wearing earplugs."

Later, when Mrs. Smith was explaining to Michael how to take care of her violets, she pointed to a big plant sitting in her living room window. "Be especially careful with this one," she said. "It's very rare because its blooms are yellow, and it was a prize winner last year. I'm working on getting it to be in full bloom in time for the local African violet show. That takes longer amounts of light than it gets from the window." She had rigged up a grow light above it and plugged that into a timer to turn it on and off.

Michael helped her put Margo's stuff into cardboard boxes and carry them over to his house. They unpacked a padded doggie bed, food and water bowls, lots of dog food, a brush, a package of rawhide bones for chewing, and a rubber squeaky toy that looked like a double-decker hamburger.

"I didn't know Margo had so much stuff," said Mom. "She should have her own suitcase."

Mrs. Smith said, "She needs her own trunk!"

"If she had a trunk," Norman said, "she'd be an elephant. A really short one."

Mrs. Smith had written down how to feed, walk, and care for the dog.

"Margo needs to go out five or six times a day," she explained to Norman. "She'll let you know when by getting your attention and going to the door. But since your yard isn't fenced in, you can't leave her out by herself unless she's tied with her leash."

Mom said, "We'll work out a schedule. On school days I get home from my part-time job about one, except Wednesdays, when I work afternoons instead. So I'll take Margo out in the middle of the day. Norman can handle most other times, and the rest of us'll take turns when he can't do it."

"I know Norman will take good care of her," Mrs. Smith told Mom, "but just in case things don't go well, here's the kennel's phone number."

"We'll do our best," Mom assured her.

As Mrs. Smith was leaving, Margo followed her to the door and whined after she left.

Norman dragged the doggie bed into the boys' room and put it between their beds.

"You can't leave it there," complained Michael. "It's too close to where we put the socks for the plants' dinner. They might grab the dog by mistake."

"They won't eat her," said Norman.

"Are you sure?" asked Michael mischievously.

Norman quickly moved the doggie bed to his side, near the end of his bed. He called, "Here, Margo!" She trotted into the boys' room. He picked up her rubber hamburger, squeaked it, and tossed it on her doggie bed. Margo pounced on the toy. *Squeak, squeak!*

Michael remarked to Norman, "That sounds better than the flutophone. Maybe you should learn to play the hamburger instead. You and Bob could start a rubber hamburger band." Norman scowled at him.

Margo carried her toy back to Norman for him to throw it again.

"Oh, yuck," he said. "It's all gooey."

Michael complained, "Doesn't she have any quiet toys?"

He soon found that life with Margo also had many other noises. She yapped when a kid came to the door selling band candy. There was also the rattle of dry dog food being poured into her metal bowl. That brought her running, with her claws clicking on the kitchen floor. She crunched her food and lapped her water loudly. *Slurp! Slurp!* She was almost as noisy an eater as Stanley and Fluffy.

Before bedtime Dad reminded Michael that it was trash night, and his turn to lug the garbage cans out to the curb. As he hauled the last one down the driveway, he saw a brown van pull into the Wards' drive on the far side of their house. It looked like a delivery van because it had no windows on its sides, but there was no sign on it. He heard the door of the Wards' attached garage roll up and then close. Back in the house, he told Mom and Dad what he had seen.

"That must be the man the Wards rented the house to," Mom said.

Norman said, "I wonder if he has any kids who'll go to our school."

The boys got ready for bed and put out the socks on the floor by each plant—dirty ones for

Stanley, clean ones for Fluffy. Margo ran over to sniff them.

"Leave those alone," said Michael. He carried her back to her bed. She licked his hand. "Stay," he ordered. To his surprise, she did. She lay with her head on her front paws, watching his every move. The boys climbed into their beds and turned out their lights. The door to the hall was open a little as usual to let some dim light in.

Michael reached out to touch Stanley, his way of saying goodnight to his plant. Stanley patted him on the shoulder. Michael was very sleepy. He was just drifting off when—*thud!* Something hit his bed. Then something wet and warm brushed his fingers. Margo was licking his hand.

He was too sleepy to get up and carry her back to her bed. He pushed her to the foot of his bed, where she was out of his way. In a moment, he was asleep.

Margo was soon asleep, too. For a long time, all was quiet except for the boys' and the dog's slow steady breathing.

Then the plants began to eat their nightly supper. Stanley reached out first. He wound a vine around one of the dirty socks set before him. Lifting it to one of his rolled-up ice-cream-cone-shaped leaves, he slowly began to suck it in. *Schlurrrrp!*

This odd noise woke Margo. She had never heard anything like it before. In the dim light from the hall, she figured out that the noise was coming from the plant. Nearby, Fluffy was twining a vine around a sock. Margo hopped off the bed and went over by Fluffy. As the plant dragged the sock along the floor, Margo clamped her jaws on the other end of the sock and tugged.

Fluffy was not about to let go of his dinner. He pulled hard on the sock. Margo growled playfully and pulled harder. Back and forth they went in a little tug-of-war—or rather, tug-of-sock. Fluffy let go. Margo trotted away with the sock, but she still wanted to play. So she came back and dropped it in front of Fluffy. The plant took hold and yanked. Margo held on.

But this time, Fluffy wanted to eat more than play. Since Margo wouldn't let go of the sock, the plant wrapped six strong vines around the dog and lifted her up to where the sock could be sucked into one of Fluffy's ice-cream-cone-shaped leaves. *Schlurrrp!* Margo let go of the sock just before it disappeared into

Fluffy. The plant quickly put the dog down on the floor.

While Stanley and Fluffy ate the rest of their dinner, Margo watched from under the far end of Norman's bed, out of vine reach.

When the plants finished their schlurping and burping, Margo tried again. She carried her hamburger to Fluffy, pressing it against a vine. Fluffy poked curiously at it and tightened the vine around it.

Squeak! went the hamburger. Startled, Fluffy quivered and dropped it. Margo tried again to get the plant to play.

Fluffy sneaked a vine closer to the toy, poked it, and picked it up. *Squeak!* went the hamburger. Fluffy hardly quivered at all this time. He tossed the toy a little way. Margo brought it back to Fluffy. They began to play—Fluffy squeaking the hamburger and tossing it away, Margo bringing it back.

Then Stanley joined the game. Margo scampered all over the room, chasing her toy. After a while, the three of them got tired of playing. Margo jumped back on Michael's bed and fell asleep.

The next morning when Michael got his bike out of the garage to go to school, he noticed that on the side of the Wards' house right next to his family's driveway, the blinds and curtains were all closed. As he rode past the front of the Wards' house, he saw that all the front windows were covered, too. He wondered what was going on in there.

Chapter 10

After school, Michael told Mom, "The guy who moved in next door had the blinds and curtains closed this morning, and now they're still closed."

"I noticed," she said.

Michael said, "I wonder what he's doing over there."

"Let's find out," decided Mom. She dumped some cookies on a paper plate, covered it with plastic wrap, and marched next door with Michael, Norman, and Bob following. She rang the front doorbell and waited. No one came. She rang again and knocked. They heard a lock turn. The door opened just a little, and a man peeked out. Michael thought he looked very ordinary—short, light brown hair, pale white skin, not very tall, wearing jeans, a T-shirt, and sneakers with dirty laces. The only odd thing about him was that he was wearing sunglasses indoors.

"Yes?" he said.

Mom introduced herself and the boys. "We just came over to welcome you to the neighborhood. We brought you some cookies."

"That's nice of you," said the man, opening the door just wide enough to take the plate. "I moved in last night and haven't gone to the grocery store yet. I'm Brett Aldrich. It's nice to meet you. I'm sorry I can't invite you in, but I didn't get any sleep last night. I'm exhausted."

"I understand," said Mom. "If you have any questions about the neighborhood, let me or my husband know."

Norman piped up, "Do you have any kids?"

"No," said Mr. Aldrich. "Thanks for the cookies." He closed the door. They heard the lock snap and a bolt click into place.

Back home, Michael said, "He seemed like he was in a hurry to get rid of us."

"Yes," agreed Mom. "But I can understand him not wanting to invite people in if he's exhausted—or if the house looks a mess." She added, "We didn't find out anything about him except his name. It was a total waste of cookies."

Michael remarked, "He said 'I' moved in, not 'we'—so he must live alone."

Norman said, "And no kids."

"He stays up late," said Bob.

"I wonder why he wears sunglasses in the house," asked Michael.

"Maybe he has an eye infection," said Mom.

Michael said, "This is a good mystery—The Case of the New Neighbor."

"Don't you dare start snooping," warned Mom. "And stay out of that yard."

"But the Wards let us run around over there all we want," complained Norman.

Mom commanded, "But they're not there now. Stay away. As my mother used to tell me when I wanted to act like Nancy Drew, M.Y.O.B. Mind your own business."

"That's no fun," whined Norman.

"I know," said Mom. "But it's safer. You can't go on other people's property if they don't want you there. That's trespassing. It's against the law. You can get arrested for it. And even if Mr. Aldrich invited you over, I wouldn't want you to go. We don't know anything about him."

"We could just sort of look around a little," said Michael. "What's wrong with that?"

"You can also get arrested for looking into people's windows," she added.

Michael said, "But in books and movies kids are always snooping around in scary yards and buildings and peeking in windows."

"Don't do it in real life," warned Mom.

"Do you think he's some kind of bad guy?" asked Michael.

"I just don't want you to take any chances," she said.

Michael said, "Well, we couldn't peek in his windows anyway because they're all covered up."

Norman felt a little jealous of Michael's success at solving his mystery of the missing book. So he got out his detective kit. He had not played with it for a long time. There was a book called *How To Be a Detective,* a magnifying glass, an ink pad for making fingerprints, a code book, and the glasses-with-nose-and-moustache disguise.

What interested him the most was a big bag of special mold-making powder. Mixed with water, it made goop to pour into the dents of footprints in soft ground. It dried quickly into hard molds of the prints.

The ground was still soft from all the rain,

so Norman and Bob looked for footprints. At this time of year, nothing was growing in the flower beds along the sides of the house, so there were plenty of muddy places to look. They found paw prints. The only human prints looked like edges or heels of sneakers. To get some good prints to make molds of, they jumped in a patch of muddy ground and carefully stepped out backwards. Norman mixed up some mold goop and poured it on. In a few minutes, they had hardened molds of the bottoms of their own sneakers.

They went in the back door, tracking mud on the kitchen floor. They showed Mom their molds. She poured them some grape juice and sat down at the table to take a closer look.

"Very clever," she said. "But how does making molds of your shoes help you detect?"

"When we find footprints," explained Norman, "we'll know if they're ours."

"But you'd already know if you've been there. You won't have to identify your own footprints."

"But," said Norman, "what if we know we haven't been there? Then we'd know somebody else was wearing our shoes."

"That's right," said Bob. "Somebody could sneak off with our sneakers."

67

Mom remarked, "I guess that's logical think-ing—sort of." She noticed the trail of muddy prints leading from the back door. "Aha!" she exclaimed. "The clue of the mysterious foot-prints leading right to your feet! Using my amazing Sherlock powers of logical thinking, I deduce that you are both wearing your own shoes. And I predict that you will get paper towels and clean up the mud as soon as you finish your grape juice." They all burst out laughing.

A couple of days later, Dad still didn't think the closed curtains next door were anything to worry about.

"He probably just doesn't want people pass-ing by to see in at night. That's not unusual. We close our bedroom curtains at night."

"But he keeps them all closed all day, too," said Michael.

Norman said, "He must have to turn his lights on in the daytime because it's dark in-side the house."

Dad remarked, "He's going to run up a big electricity bill."

Michael asked, "Why wouldn't he want day-light coming in the windows?"

Norman said, "Maybe he's a vampire!"

"Don't be silly," said Mom.

Norman insisted, "Sunlight kills vampires. That's why they don't want any."

"There's no such thing as vampires," said Dad.

Norman asked, "Did you ever see him outside in the daytime?"

"Yes," replied Mom. "As a matter of fact, I saw him outside this afternoon. He was digging in the back yard. And the sunlight didn't kill him," she added with a smile.

Norman thought that over, looking disappointed. Then he brightened up and said, "Maybe he had on some really strong sun block lotion."

"Give your imagination a rest," advised Dad.

Norman said, "Maybe he was burying stolen jewels! Or a body!"

"Stop it!" said Mom. "It's wrong to jump to conclusions without any proof and falsely accuse people—even of silly things like that. Remember how you felt when Michael accused you of taking his lost book?"

"I was really mad," recalled Norman.

"And weren't your feelings a little hurt?" asked Mom.

"Yeah."

"Then don't do that to other people."

"But what if . . ." began Norman.

"No what ifs," she said. "I saw what he was burying. It was peat moss and dried cow manure. That's what it said on the big bags of stuff he dumped on one of the Wards' flower beds. He was digging it in, mixing it with the soil to make it better for growing."

Norman was clearly disappointed. "I wished it was jewels," he said. "Then we could dig them up and be rich."

Dad reminded him, "If you found stolen jewels, we'd call the police and give them back."

"Then maybe we'd get a reward," Norman said.

Dad said, "I don't want you looking for stolen jewels."

"But what if I accidentally see some?"

"Tell me and your mother, and we'll call police."

"But what if . . ."

Dad said, "It's time to take Margo for another walk."

While Mom was making a shopping list, she said, "We need to get better prepared for emergencies. One flashlight nobody can find in a hurry isn't enough. We need flashlights for every room and extra batteries."

Michael suggested, "And radio batteries."

70

"While we're at it, we should test the smoke alarm batteries," added Dad. He used Norman's flutophone to reach the detectors on the ceilings, pressing the test buttons.

Eeeeeee, went each detector, sounding much worse than Norman playing the flutophone.

"We could have fire drills," said Norman, "like at school."

"Excellent idea," agreed Dad.

"We need more candles and matches," said Mom, adding those to her list.

Norman reminded her, "We're almost out of socks." She wrote that down. "Fudge ripple," he said. That was Fluffy's favorite flavor, white socks with brown stripes around the top. "Some strawberry, too," he said. Mom wrote down "pink."

"We should have emergency socks for plant food," he said, "in case the socks stores aren't open for a long time."

Mom said, "We should stockpile some emergency food for us, too—things that don't need a refrigerator, in case power is off for a long time. And we need glue to put the broken lamp back together."

Norman said, "I need more poster paint, all the colors, in big jars."

"What for?" asked Mom, looking suspicious.

"Artwork," replied Norman. "On paper. I want to paint some big pictures."

"Oh, all right," she decided. "I don't want to discourage your creative urges." She laughed. "Just promise you won't get any chimpanzees or elephants involved."

Dad and the boys took the shopping list to the Save-A-Lot Discount Store, where they usually bought socks because the prices were so cheap.

They returned with many bags. Unloading them in the kitchen, Dad showed off the big battery-powered camping lanterns he had bought. He turned off the lights to show how one really lit up a room.

Michael said, "This'll be good light for reading scary stories."

Norman lugged the big bag of socks to the boys' room. "Din-din," he told Fluffy. "Fudge ripple, with strawberry, for dessert tonight. Yum-yum."

Dad pulled a huge container from one of the bags. Mom looked at the label.

"You bought a gallon of glue?" she said.

"It was on sale," explained Dad. "I considered buying a glue gun, but this was a really great deal."

"What are we going to do with so much glue?" she asked. "It'll take us years to use this up."

Dad grinned. "Maybe we'll have some more power failures, and you'll break some more lamps. We'll be prepared." Mom laughed.

When he got the shattered lamp put back together, it didn't look good. The edges of some pieces had been crushed in the crash and didn't fit perfectly.

"We'll have to buy a new one," Dad decided.

"At least you tried," said Mom. "Maybe you could use all that glue to build something."

"Like what?"

"I got a book at the library by that guy on TV who builds furniture and other things in his workshop. In it there's a great wooden knickknack display box with lots of little compartments. It would take a lot of glue."

"I don't want to build a knickknack box," said Dad.

Mom said, "The boys can help. It'll be a father-son togetherness thing."

"We already have plenty of togetherness," said Dad.

"If you made a bunch of them," Mom continued, "that would use up even more glue—one for me, presents for your mother and my mother and Mrs. Smith, and some to donate to the school fund-raising craft sale."

Dad suggested, "Why don't you make them yourself?"

"Would you cut all the pieces of wood?"

"Okay," said Dad. "We can have an assembly line—I'll cut, you put them together and glue them, and the boys can paint them."

Norman said, "I want to glue. Can I glue?"

"Sure," said Mom. "I can use all the help I can get."

Chapter 11

One afternoon it was warm and dry enough for the boys to take the plants out in the backyard for extra sunlight. Michael had proven by experimenting some time ago that when the plants got more light, they ate fewer socks.

Michael left Norman to keep an eye on them while he went to Mrs. Smith's to take care of the violets. When he returned, he found that Norman had set up an art assembly line. There were about ten big pieces of paper in rows on the ground. He had filled his Water Blaster with red paint and rolled Fluffy from paper to paper, helping him aim a squirt at each one. Fluffy already knew how to use the Blaster to water himself, so he took to this kind of art right away.

While the red paint dried, Norman washed out the Blaster with the hose and loaded it with another color. They went around the papers again, squirting green, then blue, then purple. Michael got back just as Fluffy was finishing off the paintings with splats of yellow.

"This is crazy," remarked Michael as he walked around, looking at the plant's artwork.

"No, it's not," replied Norman huffily. "I'm going to be rich! I'm selling ten pictures for three hundred dollars! Apiece!"

"Nobody's going to be dumb enough to pay that," said Michael. "Who'd want to buy one of those anyway?"

"Everybody's going to want one when they find out a plant painted these!"

"Nobody's going to believe that," said Michael. "And artists are supposed to sign their names on their paintings. Fluffy can't do that. Or are you going to teach him to write 'Fluffy the Plant'?"

Norman frowned. "I don't think the chimp and the elephant could write their names, either," he said.

Mom came out the back door. Before she had gotten the door closed, Margo slipped past her and galloped around the yard. The dog ran over three paintings before Norman grabbed her.

"Bad dog!" he scolded. Margo jumped up on him, glad to see him. He held on to her until Mom got the leash.

Norman inspected the damage. In some wet spots, Margo had left smeared paw prints. Her claws had made little rips in the paper.

"She wrecked my pictures!" he howled.

Mom looked around. "Only three," she said. "You've got plenty left." She walked around, looking at them. "These are pretty good," she said. "Very colorful. You did an wonderful job."

"I helped Fluffy paint them," bragged Norman. "With my Blaster. And we didn't get any paint where it wasn't supposed to be. We were very neat."

Mom asked, "Are you sure you didn't spray paint anything accidentally?" She looked around, but the paint was mostly on the papers. Hardly any was on the grass.

"I'm glad this turned out better than the Blaster disasters you've had in the past," she said, "the times with the maple syrup and grape jelly and mustard."

Michael added, "Don't forget the chocolate syrup and liquid soap."

Norman did not look pleased to be reminded of those spectacular messes.

"Want to buy a picture?" he asked.

"How much?" asked Mom.

"Three hundred dollars?" asked Norman hopefully.

"I can't afford that," said Mom. "How about three dollars?"

"Okay," said Norman happily. "Which one do you want?"

Mom picked one with lots of yellow splatters. "I feel honored," she said, "to be the first person to buy a picture painted by a plant." She picked up her picture by one corner because it was still wet in spots, and went into the house.

Margo barked. The boys turned around to look. The new neighbor was coming toward them. This time he wasn't wearing sunglasses and didn't look as pale as before.

"Interesting paintings you've got there," he remarked.

"Hi," said Michael. Mr. Aldrich walked around, looking down at the pictures. "Good colors," he remarked. He hardly glanced at Fluffy and Stanley as he passed them to look at the rest of the pictures. He walked over near Margo. She backed away. He crouched down and held out a hand toward her. She came over, sniffed his hand, and licked his fingers. He patted her side. She liked that.

"Nice doggie," said Mr. Aldrich. "What's his name?"

"Margo," said Norman. "She's a girl dog."

"Hi, Margo," said Mr. Aldrich. She wagged her tail.

Mom came out. "I thought I heard a strange voice out here," she said. "Are you all settled?"

"Yes, no problems. It's a wonderful house. It has everything anybody could possibly need."

"How's your business going?" asked Mom.

"Fine."

"What exactly do you do?" asked Mom.

"I'm in sales."

"What kind of sales?"

"Exports and imports," he said. "Different kinds of things."

"Dealing with other countries must be interesting," said Mom.

"Very interesting," replied Mr. Aldrich. "Never a dull moment." He looked at his watch. "I have to get going. I have an appointment with a real estate agent to look at some houses. See you around." He left. Soon his van backed out of the driveway.

Mom said, "He seemed a lot friendlier this time."

Norman asked, "What's imperts?"

"Im*ports,*" she said. "Those are things from

other countries that are shipped to America for sale here. And exports are American products sold to people in other countries."

"Oh," said Norman, "I thought he said exports and imperts."

Mom added, "There's no such thing as an impert."

"There should be," said Norman. "That would be a good word."

She laughed. "It would be a good word for someone who is impertinent—like smart-mouthed or rude. Your pictures look dry now. Gather them up and bring Margo and the plants in. It looks like rain again."

As Michael rolled Stanley into the house, he thought it was odd that Mr. Aldrich had not said anything about the plants. When most people saw them for the first time, they asked what kind they were and remarked how weird they looked. Really polite people used the word "unusual."

Thunder muttered in the distance. The sky grew darker. It began to rain.

Chapter 12

Michael got used to the daily routine of going over to Mrs. Smith's house to take care of the violets. This took a while because he had to stick a finger into the soil in each pot to see whether it felt like it needed water. Too much would be as bad as not enough, and Mrs. Smith was counting on him. He peeked under the leaves of the prize plant. The little yellow buds were coming along.

Mom hurried home by one from her part-time job to take Margo out during school days, except on Wednesdays, when she worked afternoons until six. After school, Norman was supposed to take Margo for a walk before he did anything else. Then he and Bob had to put off playing detective until they practiced on their flutophones. The noises they made actually sounded like notes now. They were getting better every day.

On the few days that were not cold or rainy, Norman added taking Fluffy out for sun to his schedule. One day he took the plant out before he walked Margo.

The ground was wet, so he rolled Fluffy over on the driveway near the garage door. Although the front of the drive sloped down a little, the back part was level, so Fluffy could not accidentally roll away. Bob started looking for footprints. Norman joined in.

Mom called from the back door, "Norman! Margo needs to go for her walk!"

"I can't take her right now," he said. "I'm watching Fluffy."

"Then just take her around in the backyard. Remember, you promised Mrs. Smith you'd take good care of her." Mom brought the dog out on the leash.

Norman stood in the middle of the yard holding the leash while Margo circled him. She stopped to sniff the ground here and there. The leash wrapped around his legs. He had to turn to untangle himself.

"Hurry up and go," said Norman impatiently. Margo continued to wander, inspecting with her nose. A couple of times he thought she had found a spot to suit her, but no. Margo kept looking. Bob had gone off around the side of the house.

"Make up your mind," said Norman. He remarked to Fluffy, "I'm glad plants don't have to go to the bathroom."

Margot finally chose a spot on the grass next to the drive and squatted.

Just then Bob yelled, "Hey, Norman! Come quick!"

Norman thought it must be important if Bob wanted him to hurry. He wrapped one of Fluffy's vines around the loop of the leash.

"Hold this a second," he told Fluffy. "I'll be right back." He ran down the drive. Bob was at the front edge of the Wards' lawn next to the drive. He had found a footprint in a muddy spot.

As Norman knelt to look closely, he heard two noises behind him—paws scrabbling on cement and skateboard wheels rolling.

Down the drive trotted Margo, followed by Fluffy, still holding the leash. Although the dog was pulling the plant, it looked like Fluffy was taking Margo for a walk. Norman and Bob grabbed them just before they reached the street.

Bob often came along on Margo's walks. Because the dog stopped to sniff at lots of places along the way, they pretended she was a bloodhound following a trail.

They decided to call themselves The Detective Club and not let anybody else join. They used the ink pad in the kit to make their own fingerprints on paper. Mom and Dad also let Norman take their fingerprints. Bob persuaded his parents, too. They tried to take Margo's pawprints, but she wouldn't cooperate.

The junior detectives also had a good time running around looking at things through the magnifying glass and saying "Aha!" They wrote secret messages in code and wrote down license numbers of all the cars, vans, and trucks in the neighborhood.

Because they were running low on mold goop powder, Norman decided to experiment with something else. He poured most of the gallon of glue into his Water Blaster, made a footprint in damp ground, and pumped glue into it. But the glue soaked in and dried with a bunch of dirt stuck to it.

Next, Norman and Bob decided to make shoe prints like fingerprints. They painted the soles of their shoes with poster paint and quickly, before the paint dried, pressed the shoes onto sheets of paper. Norman was fascinated by the patterns made by different kinds of sneakers. Soon they had a complete set of prints from the shoes worn most often by both of their families.

Now, when Norman found a footprint in the yard, he could check his stack of green, purple, and orange prints to see whose it was.

Norman told Mom, "You were outside by the bathroom window today."

She looked surprised. "Why, yes," she replied. "I was washing the window. How did you know? You were in school all day."

"Just detecting," he said mysteriously.

"That's a very good deduction," said Mom. "How did you guess?"

"From clues."

"What clues?"

"I'm not telling."

"You're an amazing detective, all right."

Norman beamed with pride. Mom went outside to look at the window and noticed the footprints.

"Aha!" she said.

Later, Norman walked around the house to see if there were any other new footprints. Outside the window of the boys' room he saw part of a sneaker print. But the outside of that window was not clean like the bathroom window.

He went inside to amaze Mom again. "You looked in our room window today and didn't wash it."

"No, I only did one side of the house today. I might do that side tomorrow."

"But you looked in our window."

"No. Why would I? There's nothing much to see except the plants standing there. Any footprints you found there must belong to Michael or your father."

Norman asked, "How did you know I found footprints?"

"I'm the mother of a detective," said Mom, "so I know these things. Besides, I used to read Nancy Drew books. Maybe Bob came around looking for you and looked in."

Bob arrived a few minutes later.

Norman tried to amaze him. "You looked in my window," he said.

"No," replied Bob. "Why would I look in your window? You're right here."

Mom said, "When you match it up with the family shoe prints, then you'll know who it was."

Norman mixed up some goop and made a mold of the foot print under the window. It was part of a sneaker heel. He and Bob compared it to all the prints they had. It didn't match any of them.

"This is sort of creepy," said Norman. Just then Michael came in. Norman told him about the mysterious print. Michael went through the shoeprints himself. He was sure Norman and Bob must have made a mistake.

"You're right," he finally agreed. "This doesn't match any of our shoes. So the logical explanation is . . ." He stepped to the window and pulled the curtains shut. "This means somebody's been spying on us!"

They told Mom. She called Dad at work to tell him.

"It could be anybody," he said. "It doesn't necessarily mean anything creepy is going on. But just in case, make sure you keep the doors and windows locked. I know we try to do that all the time, but once in a while we get careless."

That evening, when it was getting dark, Mom went from room to room and closed all the curtains. Dad decided to leave the outdoor light by the front door on all night. The next evening he bought a couple of lights with motion sensors that turned on automatically if someone came within a certain distance. He installed them by the back door and on the side of the house where the boys' window was.

Norman went to the basement to pump the glue out of his Blaster back into the container. But on the way down the stairs, he got a great idea.

He went back up and asked Mom, "When are we going to glue knickknack boxes?"

"Soon," she replied without looking up from the book she was reading. "Right after we buy the wood and your father cuts it up."

Norman said, "I'm ready to glue."

"Good," said Mom, reading on.

Norman went back down to the basement, feeling very pleased with himself. He had invented a glue gun and it didn't cost anything. Mom and Dad were really going to be surprised.

He decided to glue some wood scraps together for practice. But he was used to pumping big blasts of water and paint, not little squirts of glue. Every time he tried, too much glue came out all over the worktable. Some dripped over the edge onto the floor where he was standing. Norman kept trying. He had a whole heap of wood scraps, so he stuck them all together to use up the spreading puddle of glue.

When he needed more wood scraps and turned to go get them, he almost fell over. His sneakers were stuck to the floor. He tried to untie his shoelaces, but they were glued, too. He managed to pull his feet out and ran upstairs in his socks to get a table knife to pry his shoes loose.

Mom called, "Norman, what are you doing?"

"Nothing," he replied. He scurried back to the basement and freed his shoes. Before he went to bed, he cut the laces out with scissors and put in new ones.

Chapter 13

By the front corner of the house nearest the Wards' was a stand of thick bushes. When the boys were younger, they used to play in there, pretending they were in a cave or a fort.

Now Norman and Bob began using this little hideout to spy on Mr. Aldrich in the late afternoon or early evening. They didn't do it very long at a time because they got bored watching nothing happen. Once in a while they saw him come or go in his van.

They got very excited when a man carrying a large flat box arrived. But they soon detected that he was just delivering pizza.

They were about to give up and go kick a soccer ball around when another man drove up and rang Mr. Aldrich's doorbell. This stranger was not carrying anything. When the door opened, they heard the man say, "I'm Reynolds. We spoke on the phone last night."

"Yes, come in," said Mr. Aldrich. The visitor went inside.

Norman said, "This is great! A mysterious stranger! I wonder who he is!" He wrote down the license number.

Just then they heard footsteps and Margo nosed her way in behind the bushes to join them.

Michael, who was holding her leash, said, "Mom said you should take Margo for a walk."

"You take her," replied Norman. "We're busy detecting."

"Detecting what?" said Michael scornfully. "You don't have a clue about how to detect."

"We do too have a clue," protested Bob. "A mysterious stranger just went in that house."

"Move over," said Michael. He squeezed himself into the small space behind the bushes.

"Stop it!" said Norman. "You're squashing me and Margo!"

"Then move over more! Do you know what he's doing there?"

"No, he just said, 'I'm Reynolds. We spoke on the phone.' "

Michael thought that over. "Could he be a pizza guy?"

"No, he wasn't carrying a pizza box."

Bob said, "Maybe he's selling band candy."

"No," said Norman. "For band candy they always make you wait outside while they go get their money. Like with pizza."

"Oh, yeah," said Bob. "That's true."

Norman complained to Michael, "Your elbow is sticking in my ribs!"

"Then move your ribs out of the way!" They heard the neighbor's door open.

"Shhh!" warned Norman. The mysterious stranger came out carrying a brown cardboard box about three feet long and two feet high.

"Thanks, Fred," he said to Mr. Aldrich, who was standing in the doorway. "I'm very pleased to get this. Let me know when you have something else I'm looking for."

"Of course," said Mr. Aldrich. "I'm sure we'll be doing business together again soon. I'll be in touch." The stranger gently laid the box in the trunk of his car and left. Mr. Aldrich closed his door.

Norman said, "He bought something from him. I wonder what was in that box."

Michael said, "The stranger called him Fred. He told us his name was Brett."

Bob said, "Fred must be his nickname."

Michael said, "He must be using a fake name—an alias. Maybe this proves he really is a crook!"

"A real crook?" said Bob.

"I bet I know what was in that box," said Norman. "Stolen jewels!"

Michael said, "He wouldn't need that big a box for jewels."

Norman said, "Maybe they're really big jewels!"

Dad came around the side of the house. "Boys!" he called. "Where are you?" He stopped next to the bushes, not seeing them.

"Don't look here," said Norman's voice from near Dad's knees. "We're detecting. Pretend like you don't know we're here."

Dad told him, "That's enough detecting for this evening. Bob, your mother just called to tell you to come home."

"Okay," said Bob. He crawled out of the bushes. "See you," he told Norman, and headed off down the street.

"Where's Michael?" Dad asked. "He went out to take Margo for a walk."

"He tried to make me do it," complained Norman. He came out from behind the bushes, followed by Margo and Michael.

"What is this?" asked Dad. "A detecting convention in the bushes? What're you all up to in there?"

"Just spying," explained Norman.

"But not trespassing," added Michael. "We stayed on our own property. We just found out Mr. Aldrich is probably a crook."

"Let's all take Margo for a walk," suggested Dad. "Tell me all about this."

After they told him all about the stranger's visit to Mr. Aldrich and how it proved their neighbor was a crook, Dad said, "You're doing it again. Stop jumping to wild conclusions."

The next afternoon, Chad and Michael went to the public library to work on a school report they were doing together. After a librarian helped them find the information they needed, they took notes and photocopied some materials. Before checking out the books they needed, they looked at the rack where their favorite series was kept. Michael picked up *The Return of the Evil Ooze* and *The Revenge of the Werewolf Piano Teacher*. Chad also found a couple he had not read yet.

"I'm finished with *The Curse of the Evil Ooze*," said Michael, "if you want to borrow it."

"Great," said Chad.

As they were leaving, Michael stopped to look at a display.

Chad said, "I have to get going. I'll call you tonight."

Coming out of the library a few minutes later, Michael noticed someone who looked familiar at the far end of the parking lot. About twenty cars away, a man who looked like Mr. Aldrich was standing alone, holding a large blue shopping bag by its handles and looking around.

Michael ducked back inside the glass library doors to wait and see what Mr. Aldrich was doing there. He saw a woman get out of a car in the next row and walk toward him. He handed her the bag. She looked in it, inspected the contents, and handed him an envelope. She took the bag back to her car and drove away. Mr. Aldrich strolled over to the nearby bus stop and sat down on the bench there.

Why hadn't he driven his van, Michael wondered. And what was in that shopping bag?

A voice on the library P.A. system announced, "We'll be closing in fifteen minutes at six o'clock." Michael hadn't realized it was so late. As he unlocked his bike from the rack, he saw Mr. Aldrich get on the bus.

When Michael got home, the wonderful smell

of meat loaf hit him in the nose. The family was sitting down to dinner.

"You're just in time," Mom said. "Did you and Chad find everything you needed?"

"Yeah. And I saw Mr. Aldrich in the library parking lot. He had a big blue shopping bag that he gave to some lady, and she gave him an envelope. But he wasn't driving his van. He took the bus. He must be up to something."

Dad said, "Maybe his van's in for repairs."

Norman said, "I bet the bag was full of stolen jewels!"

"Stop jumping to wild conclusions," said Mom. "There's probably a perfectly logical explanation for what he was doing there. Pass the carrots."

Michael remarked, "Everything he does looks suspicious."

Mom said, "When he was over here this afternoon, he didn't look suspicious at all."

Michael was surprised. "What did he come over for?" he asked.

"No particular reason," explained Mom. "I was in the backyard talking to Norman. He was out there with Margo and the plants. Mr. Aldrich came out his back door and saw us. He walked over and said hello."

"What did he talk about?" asked Dad.

96

"The weather. All the rain we've been having. I asked if the Wards' pump was working all right. He said it kicks on just fine every time heavy rain starts leaking in. I asked him about his search for a house to buy. He said he's looked at quite a few but hasn't found what he wants."

Norman said, "He gave Margo some doggie treats."

Dad asked, "What kind of house is he looking for?"

"When I started to ask him about that," Mom said, "he looked at his watch and said he had to go. He was expecting an important phone call."

"It must have been that lady telling him what time to meet in the parking lot," deduced Michael.

"No," said Mom. "You saw him there before he came over here."

"No," said Michael. "I saw him there just before I came home."

"Did you stop at Chad's on the way?"

"No, I didn't stop anywhere."

"Well, when he left here, he said he was expecting the phone call at five-forty-five. I looked at my watch because I wanted to check the oven at ten of six to see if the meat loaf was done. He left here about five-forty-four."

"That can't be," said Michael. "Right after the library announced it was closing at six in fifteen minutes, he was getting on the bus at the parking lot."

Dad said, "Then it couldn't have been him."

"But I thought it was," said Michael.

"Did you see him up close?"

"No. He was at the other side of the lot. I didn't go closer because I didn't want him to see me."

Dad said, "It's easy to mistake someone for somebody else at a distance. I've done that myself a few times."

"Then," said Norman, "some other guy sold the stolen jewels to that lady."

Mom told him, "We don't know what was in the bag, or who those people were. All we know is that Mr. Aldrich wasn't there. As you detectives like to say, he has an alibi witness—actually two—you and me. Three, if you count Margo. He was with us at the time of the crime. Except there probably wasn't any crime."

"Five alibis," said Norman. "Counting Fluffy and Stanley."

"Okay, five," agreed Mom. "Pass the gravy."

Michael felt like a complete fool for making such a big mistake. But even though Mr. Aldrich hadn't been in the library lot, he was still convinced that the neighbor was very suspicious.

"Come on," said Dad to the boys after dinner. "Get your jackets. We're all going shopping."

Michael sighed. "Do I have to go?"

"Sure," said Mom. "After the grocery store, we're going shopping for a new living room lamp."

"I don't want to go," replied Michael. "I want to stay home and read my library book. And Chad's going to call me. We have to talk about our report."

"All right," agreed Dad. "We won't be gone long." He turned on the front outside light.

Norman stood by the front door, ready to go, with Margo on her leash.

"The dog's not going," said Mom.

"Margo wants to go for a ride," said Norman.

"You'll have to stay in the car with her. We can't take her into stores."

Norman unclipped the leash from her collar. "You have to stay home," he told Margo. The dog raced back to the boys' room and jumped on Michael's bed.

Mom reminded Michael, "Lock the doors when we leave. Don't invite anybody in. If you answer the phone, don't tell strangers we're not here. And don't scare yourself silly with that book."

The front door banged. Car doors slammed. Michael heard the car backing out. He made sure the front door was locked. Eager to get to his book, he hurried down the hall, flopped on his bed, and kicked off his shoes. Stanley and Fluffy stood still as they usually did at this time. The dog snuggled up against his feet. He opened *The Return of the Evil Ooze* and began to read aloud: "Chapter One. I will never forget that cold November day. If I had known what lay ahead, I never would have gotten off the plane in Scotland to meet my father the archeologist and his new trusted assistant, Hugo."

The plants leaned forward a little. Michael was interrupted by the phone ringing. He went across the hall to Mom and Dad's room to answer it. Just as he got there, the answering machine clicked on and recited its instruction to leave a message. Michael decided to wait and hear if it was Chad before he answered. But the caller hung up without saying anything. Chad would have spoken up. Michael went back to his book.

Four chapters later, the evil ooze was bubbling up the winding stairs of the castle tower where Kevin was cornered once again. Margo had fallen asleep. The plants stood motionless. The house was silent.

Michael felt hungry for a little after-dinner snack. He got up and started out of the bedroom. He wasn't sure what alerted him, but he sensed something was not quite right.

He thought he had heard something. He stood still in the hall and listened. He felt his heart pounding. Don't be silly, he told himself. There's nothing there. No ghosts. No creepy intruders. Reading *The Return of the Evil Ooze* was getting to him. But he did not move. He listened.

There it was again! The sound was so faint he could hardly hear it. But now he was sure what it was. Someone—or something—was moving through the kitchen.

Chapter 14

Michael didn't know what to do. Tiptoe back to the bedroom and hide under the bed? Climb out the bedroom window and run to a neighbor's to call the police? Make a run for Mom and Dad's room to call from there and then climb out their window? Wake up Margo and hope she would bark and scare away whatever was creeping through the kitchen? Or lock himself in the bathroom and wait for Mom and Dad to come home? No, that wouldn't work. Dad had taken the lock off the bathroom door.

Then he realized that whoever—or whatever—was in the kitchen wasn't trying to be quiet. He—or it—must think no one was home. The footsteps sounded like they were heading into the dining room. Then Michael heard

Squeak! The intruder had stepped on Margo's hamburger.

Frantic, Michael saw Norman's flutophone on the hall table. He grabbed it, climbed on the chair next to the table, and used the flutophone to reach the test button on the smoke alarm. *Screeeeeee!* That woke Margo. She leaped off the bed and ran down the hall to get away from the piercing sound.

Michael put his free hand over one ear, but it did no good. The noise was painful. He released the test button for a moment and listened. Someone was going fast through the kitchen and knocked over a chair. Michael blew a few toots on the flutophone, hoping that sounded like a burglar alarm. *Screech, squonk, screech.* Stanley and Fluffy both tried to get out of the boys' room at the same time and got stuck in the doorway in a plant traffic jam.

Michael stopped to listen again. In the sudden quiet, he heard the back door close.

He tiptoed to the kitchen door and pushed it open just enough to see in. The light over the sink was on. The room was empty except for Margo, who sat calmly on her haunches looking totally undisturbed.

Keeping low, Michael hurried to the window over the sink and peeked between the closed curtains. There was nothing to see—just darkness. The motion light on the back of the house was not on. But how could that be? Whoever had come in the back door or gone out the same way must have triggered the sensor. Why hadn't the light gone on?

To his horror, Michael realized that if the prowler had not gone out the back door, he could still be in the house.

Headlights lit up the garage door. Mom and Dad were back. Michael ran out to the car. He quickly told what had happened.

Dad told everybody to wait in the car with the doors locked while he ran inside to call 911 from the kitchen phone. Then he joined them in the car.

In a few minutes, a police car pulled into the drive behind them. One of the two policemen was Officer Tim. They searched the house to make sure the prowler was not still there. The other officer went around to the neighbors to ask if anyone had seen anything. After Michael told Officer Tim what happened, the family checked to see if anything had been stolen, but nothing was missing.

Officer Tim noticed *The Return of the Evil Ooze* on Michael's bed. "When my kid reads those books," he said, "he doesn't want to be home alone. Are you sure you heard those noises? It wasn't just the book getting you spooked, was it? Our imaginations can play tricks on us sometimes."

"I'm sure," replied Michael.

Officer Tim inspected the sensor light by the back door. "Here's why it didn't go on," he said. "The bulb's gone. There's no sign of a break-in. Was the door unlocked?"

Michael felt embarrassed when he admitted he had forgotten to check the back door.

Dad said, "Who would steal our light bulb?"

"Somebody who didn't want to be seen," said Mom.

Norman said, "I think it was the guy next door." Officer Tim patiently listened to the boys' suspicions, although he wasn't writing anything down.

His partner returned and reported that the neighbors had not seen or heard anything.

"Did you talk to the guy next door?" asked Michael.

"Yes, he said he was asleep on the living room couch. He looked like he just woke up."

Several neighbors came over to find out what was going on. After everyone left, Dad locked the back door. They left a light on in every room all night. It started raining again.

*   *   *

The next day was Wednesday. Since Mom wouldn't be home until six, the boys called her at work to let her know they were home from school. It was a warm afternoon, so they rolled the plants out. The yard was muddy again from last night's rain.

Michael said, "Let's put them on the drive so their wheels won't sink into the lawn." The wheels had already picked up mud and left brown tracks on the light gray concrete drive.

"I'll watch the plants first while you walk Margo," Michael said. Norman brought the dog out on her leash. From next door, they heard the garage door open. A motor started. Norman strolled down the driveway with Margo and watched Mr. Aldrich drive away in his van.

"He's gone," Norman reported back to Michael. "I'm going over there to look in the garage window." He tied the end of Margo's leash around the handle of the back door. He put her hamburger toy beside her.

"You'd better not," warned Michael.

"It's okay," said Norman. "He can't catch me. He's not there." He ran into Mr. Aldrich's yard and disappeared around the back of the garage.

When he did not come back right away, Michael followed, after making sure the plants were not within vine reach of anything they could grab onto to move. They were on the flat part of the drive so they could not accidentally roll away.

Michael found Norman staring into a window that was almost hidden behind a wide clump of bushes.

"Hurry up! Come away from there," he urged his brother.

"In a minute," said Norman. "I'm looking at everything."

"What's in there? Move over!" Michael pushed through the bushes, elbowed Norman aside and cupped his hands around his face to see better into the dim garage.

He saw a well-organized place, the way the Wards always kept it, not like the jumble of stuff in their own garage. A power mower, clean and shining, stood in one corner. Some yard tools, a shovel, a rake, and pruning shears hung on a wall. On a workbench sat some big bags marked Peat Moss and Dried Cow Manure.

"Just gardening stuff," said Michael. "Come on. Let's get out of here before he comes back."

"Wait, I'm still looking," said Norman. "There might be something suspicious."

"There aren't any stolen jewels," joked Michael. "Come on. We shouldn't leave Stanley and Fluffy out by themselves. Or Margo either."

The plants and the dog were patiently waiting right where they had left them.

"See?" said Norman. "They can take care of themselves for a few minutes."

Stanley tapped Michael on the shoulder and pointed to his pot to let him know he needed watering. He checked Fluffy, too.

"They both need water," Michael told Norman. "Go fill up your Blaster."

"No, it's got other stuff in it," said Norman. The hose was disconnected from the outdoor faucet and neatly coiled up, so he got a pail from the garage and went around the far corner of the house to fill it at the faucet.

Michael went in to get some paper towels to clean the mud off the plants' skateboard wheels. He thought it would be easier to wipe off while it was still gooey. He opened the refrigerator to get some grape juice and took a swig from the bottle because he was in a hurry.

Moments later, when he came back outside, the plants were not in the driveway. He went around the corner of the house, where Norman was almost through filling the pail.

"Where'd you put the plants?" he asked.

"Nowhere," said Norman. "They're in the drive."

"No, they're not. Quit kidding. Where'd you put them?"

Norman ran to where the plants had been.

"Oh no!" said Norman. "They must have got rolling somehow." Margo was still tied to the back door handle, so she couldn't have taken them for a walk.

The boys ran down the drive to the street and looked both ways to see which way the plants had gone. But the street was deserted. No people. No vehicles. And no runaway plants.

"They couldn't have rolled out of sight that fast," Michael pointed out.

"What could have happened?" asked Norman, looking panicky. "They have to be here somewhere! Fluffy!" he yelled. "Where are you?"

Michael ran back to look for clues. The muddy wheels had to have left some tracks that would show which way the plants had rolled.

But the only muddy tracks were the ones that led to where the plants had been standing in the middle of the drive. Stanley and Fluffy had not rolled away. They had just dis-appeared.

"Where could they have rolled to?" asked Norman.

"Nowhere," replied Michael. He tried to calm down and think like Sherlock Holmes.

"The mud tracks show that they didn't roll in any direction on the drive," he observed out loud. "So if they didn't do that, then there's only one way they could have gone."

"Where?" asked Norman, looking baffled.

"Up," said Michael. "I know it doesn't make any sense, but they must have gone straight up." He looked up at the sky and around at the nearby roofs, as if he expected Stanley and Fluffy to be hovering somewhere overhead. But they weren't.

"That's silly," said Norman. "They can't fly."

"Right," agreed Michael. "So they had to be lifted by someone—or something."

Norman looked horrified. "Beamed up?" he exclaimed. "By a space ship? How can that be?"

"It can't," said Michael. "There has to be a logical explanation."

Norman kept guessing: "A helicopter grabbed them?"

"No. A helicopter makes a lot of noise and wind. We didn't hear anything. Besides, a helicopter couldn't come and go that fast. We only left the plants alone a couple of minutes."

Norman said, "The only other thing I can think of is a giant. Like in *Jack and the Beanstalk.*"

Michael sighed. "Have you seen any big beanstalks around here lately? I think we would have noticed."

Norman said, "They couldn't lift themselves up in the sky, and they're heavy. It had to be something big and strong. And quiet. Aha! A pterodactyl!"

Michael scowled at him. "Get serious!" Norman crinkled his forehead to show he was thinking very hard.

"Aha!" he said.

"Now what!"

"People!" exclaimed Norman. "People picked them up and carried them away. And their shoes didn't have mud on them so they didn't leave any tracks."

Michael was astounded. Norman, the expert pest and bumbling detective, who had never read Sherlock Holmes, had figured out the only possible solution.

"They've been purloined!" exclaimed Norman.

"Now we have to deduce which way they were carried," said Michael. The boys looked all around. There were no clues. Not a leaf. Not a stem. Not a footprint. Not even a gum wrapper.

Michael was starting to feel panicky. The longer they stood around trying to figure out what happened, the farther away the plants were being taken.

He said, "To get away that fast in that little a time, they would have to use a van or truck. But we didn't hear any motor." He decided, "So if they didn't use a van or truck, they couldn't have gotten very far from here when we started looking. They could have had enough time to hide Stanley and Fluffy somewhere nearby," said Michael, turning to look at the house next door.

"Mr. Aldrich must have sneaked back!" said Norman. "Let's check his garage again." He took off running.

Michael followed. Keeping low, they stopped under the garage window.

"Be careful," whispered Michael. "We don't want him to see us." Slowly they raised their heads to the windowsill and peered in.

But Mr. Aldrich had not come back. The van was not there. Neither were Stanley and Fluffy.

Chapter 15

The boys hurried back to their own yard.

Michael said, "So somebody else took them and hid them nearby. Maybe they're planning to come back after dark and haul them away when no one can see them. Like in the middle of the night. Maybe they hid the plants in plain sight like the purloined letter. And we just don't see them."

Margo was still sitting calmly by the back door.

"I'm glad they didn't take Margo, too," said Norman. He patted her side. She rolled over to have her tummy rubbed.

Then Michael recognized a clue that might be very important.

"You know, when we didn't hear any helicopters or vans or cars—" he began.

Norman interrupted, "Or pterodactyls."

Michael continued, "There was one other thing we didn't hear."

"What?"

"Margo didn't bark. She usually barks at strangers. So it must have been somebody she knows." He turned to look at the house next door.

Norman said, "Like Mr. Aldrich. But he's not home." Then he recalled, "You know, while the water was running, I think I heard her hamburger squeak."

They looked all over. Margo's hamburger had disappeared, too.

As they stood talking, Michael noticed a little twitch of a curtain in the kitchen window on the nearest side of Wards' house. Were they being watched?

He turned his back to the window. "I saw a curtain move," he whispered. "Mr. Aldrich isn't there, but somebody else is. Whoever it is could have taken Stanley and Fluffy. They must be in the Wards' house."

They heard Mr. Aldrich's garage door roll up. His van pulled up the drive and into the garage.

"Come on," whispered Michael. He crawled

behind the hideout bushes. Norman squashed himself in behind Michael.

"Do you think whoever peeked out can see us?" whispered Norman. Michael noticed that Norman's red shirt would be easy to spot, even in the thick bushes.

"Go change your shirt," he told him. "Put on green or brown—something that'll blend in. And bring Dad's binoculars."

Norman made a dash for the back door. Michael kept an eye on all the side windows. Nothing happened. Norman soon returned in a huge brown and green camouflage T-shirt, one of Dad's that hung down past his knees. He wore a baseball cap pulled low over his eyes and his detective kit glasses with the funny nose and moustache. Dad's binoculars hung from a strap around his neck.

Michael ignored this unusual costume and grabbed the binoculars.

"Let go," protested Norman. "You're choking me with the strap."

"Quiet," said Michael. "I think the curtain just moved again. I'm trying to focus on it. There! I got a good close-up."

"What do you see?" asked Norman impatiently.

"Nothing's happening. Wait. It's moving again. Just a little."

"Are you sure they can't see us?" asked Norman.

"Probably not."

"But what if they can?"

"Shhh. The curtain's opening a little." Were they going to see the other person lurking over there?

"I'm starting to see something," said Michael.

"A face?"

"No, not a face."

"Fingers?" asked Norman excitedly.

"No, I think it's . . . wait a minute . . . yes!"

"What? What?" said Norman.

"It's thin and green. I think it's the tip of a vine!"

"Fluffy and Stanley are in there!" exclaimed Norman.

"They must be," agreed Michael. "No other plants would be fooling with the curtains. They must have heard our voices near the window and tried to signal to us."

They dashed back into the house to figure out what to do.

"We have to rescue them," said Norman, taking off his disguise glasses, hat and binoculars.

Michael said, "We need a master plan. First,

we have to get in there somehow. But we can't trespass. And if we did, Mr. Aldrich would probably catch us. So we'll have to go in the front door."

"Sneak in the front door?" asked Norman.

"No! We'll ring the bell and tell him we came to sell him something."

"Like what?"

"Have you still got your band candy bar from the ones Mom bought?"

"I ate half of it."

"We can't sell him half a candy bar. We have to think of something else." He started looking around the kitchen. "Here's my master plan."

"Wait," said Norman. "What about *my* master plan?"

"You don't have one," replied Michael.

"Well, I could think one up."

"We don't have time for you to think," said Michael. He sighed. "Here's *our* master plan."

"Okay," said Norman. "What is it?

Michael said, "We'll be Stanley and Fluffy."

Norman replied, "We can't look like plants no matter how hard we try."

"That's not what I meant," said Michael. As he opened cupboards, looking for something to sell, he explained, "We tell him those are our names. He doesn't remember our real names.

We talk real loud so the plants can hear us saying their names. When they hear our voices calling them, they'll start acting up and try to get to us. That'll get Mr. Aldrich confused, I hope, and we can run in and take the plants out real fast."

They quickly practiced what they were going to do. Norman remembered his glue gun and ran down the basement to get it in case it might come in handy. They hurried next door before they lost their nerve.

Michael rang the doorbell. "Now don't forget what you're supposed to say," he warned Norman.

Mr. Aldrich did not come to the door. Michael rang again. They waited some more.

"We have to show him we're not going away," said Michael. He rang the bell, pounded on the door, and yelled, "Mr. Aldrich! Mr. Aldrich!" He kept ringing and pounding.

Finally, they heard the lock turn and the bolt slide. The door opened just a little. Mr. Aldrich peered out. He was holding his sunglasses in one hand and did not look glad to see them.

"Yes?" he said. "What do you want?"

"Remember us?" said Michael loudly. "I'm STANLEY!" he yelled, raising his voice on the name. "From next door. And this is my brother FLUFFY!"

Mr. Aldrich looked down at the shorter boy wearing a camouflage T-shirt so long he appeared to be wearing a funny-looking dress.

"Your name is Fluffy?" he said.

"Yeah," said Norman, glaring up at him. "It's my nickname."

"Amazing," said Mr. Aldrich. "Why are you here?"

"We're selling band candy," said Michael. "To raise money for the band."

"What band is that?" asked Mr. Aldrich. "You two don't look old enough to be in a high school band."

"It's a flutophone band," explained Norman. "At Edison Elementary."

Mr. Aldrich looked at his watch, as if he were in a hurry. "Okay. I'll take two."

Michael held up a handful of breakfast snack bars.

"That's candy?" asked Mr. Aldrich.

"It's sort of breakfast candy," said Michael. He was starting to feel frantic. Norman had missed his cue, so he did what he had to do. "FLUFFY!" he yelled. "What are you doing?"

"Oh," said Norman, suddenly recalling his part. He kicked Michael in the shin and kept kicking him, not very hard. "STANLEY!" yelled Norman, "where are you? STANLEY!"

"He's right there," said Mr. Aldrich. "You're kicking him." He opened the door wider and reached out to grab Norman, but Norman sidestepped out of his reach and pumped some big splats of glue in the direction of Mr. Aldrich's feet.

"FLUFFY!" yelled Michael. "STANLEY!"

Mr. Aldrich stared at these two boys who seemed to have gone completely wacko on his doorstep. "What's this goo?" he asked, looking down at what he was stepping in, which was also oozing all over his shoelaces. With all the commotion, he hadn't heard skateboard wheels rolling up behind him and leaves rustling. He looked very surprised when strong vines wrapped around his ankles and bound his arms to his sides. Since he was no longer holding the door, it was jerked wide open from behind.

"Stanley!" said Michael. "Am I ever glad to see you!"

"Where's Fluffy?" asked Norman.

Michael hesitated. Should he run home to call the police or go in and use the Wards' phone? Stanley had Mr. Aldrich well wrapped up. But where was Fluffy?

Norman was furious. He yelled at Mr. Aldrich, "You plant stealer, you . . . you . . ." He paused, trying to think of something worse to call him. "You purloiner!" he yelled.

Mr. Aldrich, wriggling to try to get loose, replied calmly, "Help me get these vines off. I didn't steal this plant. I saw it left out in your drive. You weren't around. I'd heard on the radio another big storm was coming, so I took it inside to protect it. Hey, my feet are stuck!"

"Hah!" said Norman. "Where's my plant!"

"I only saw one," said Mr. Aldrich. "That's all I brought in."

"Liar," said Norman. "Fluffy!" he yelled. "Where are you?"

From somewhere in the house they heard a sound both boys recognized—the squeak of Margo's hamburger.

Norman squeezed past Mr. Aldrich and Stanley.

"Fluffy, keep squeaking!" he shouted. "I'll find you!"

Michael rushed in after him. The squeaking seemed to be coming from the kitchen. But Norman had stopped in the living room. He was staring at the reason why Mr. Aldrich had kept the windows covered.

Chapter 16

They had been in this house many times, but it looked very different now. In the living and dining rooms, the furniture had been moved aside next to the walls. The floor was covered with plastic sheets. The rooms were so brightly lit it made Michael squint. It was like a sunny day indoors.

Frameworks holding large lights had been rigged up. Basking under them were at least a hundred plants—many kinds and sizes.

In this secret greenhouse, Michael saw some that he thought were probably orchids because he had seen pictures of plants like them in books. Many others he did not recognize, but one he definitely did know. He had seen the plant and its pot every day. It was Mrs. Smith's prize violet. Mr. Aldrich must have stolen it today. He was in the stolen rare plants business!

While Michael looked around, Norman, in response to another squeak, opened the kitchen door. He found Fluffy boxed into a corner by a large heavy table. The plant was leaning against it but could not move it. Norman was so glad to see his plant that he did not notice that the door which led to the dining room was just swinging closed.

He put his Blaster down to try to move the heavy table, but it would not budge. One end of the table also blocked the door to the garage.

He was about to yell to Michael to come help him move the table to free Fluffy. But Michael yelled first: "Run! Run! Get help!"

Since he couldn't get the back door open, Norman ran into the living room. Michael was kicking and struggling and firmly held from behind by Mr. Aldrich. Why had Stanley let him go? Norman decided to make a dash for the front door. Then he thought maybe he could jump on Mr. Aldrich's back, hold on around his neck, and kick him until he let go of Michael. While he tried to get up the nerve to do this, he looked around for Stanley. The plant was still by the front door. And his vines were still wrapped around Mr. Aldrich. There were two of him!

"Clone!" gasped Norman.

Michael, who had not gotten a good look at the one who had sneaked in from the dining room and grabbed him from behind, kept yelling, "Run! Run!"

But the Mr. Aldrich holding Michael dragged him, still kicking, toward the coat closet near the front door. He shoved Michael into the closet and turned a key in the lock. Then he went after Norman. He had to chase him around the room three times but finally caught him by the back of his jacket. Norman slipped out of his jacket and kept running, but the man caught him by the back of his shirt and shoved him into the closet, too.

Michael put an arm around Norman in the dark. "Are you okay?" he whispered.

"Yeah," replied Norman. "Are you?"

"Yeah. We have to think of a master plan to get out of here fast. But I can't think of anything." They sat quietly, huddled together.

Norman said, "I never saw a real clone before!"

"What?"

"The one who grabbed you. He looks exactly alike."

"They must be twins," said Michael. "Identical ones."

"Oh," said Norman. "Twins. Yeah."

Michael continued, "Then it *was* him at the library. Or one of him. And that explains the two first names and how he took our plants when we knew he wasn't home. If they don't let people see them together, nobody knows there's two of them. They can be in two places at once anytime they want an alibi."

They heard thumping outside the closet door. "Hurry up," said one of the twins. "Get these vines off me! We have to change plans and move out right now. We can't wait until tonight."

The other replied, "I'm trying but these vines won't unwind. It's like they're holding on on purpose."

His brother said, "Get the pruning shears from the garage and cut them off. And then help me get these shoes off. They're stuck to the floor."

Michael whispered, "Oh, no!" He didn't want Stanley's vines chopped, even though the plant could grow more. Maybe if the Aldrich Stanley held prisoner was let loose, the two crooks would leave. After that he and Norman would figure out how to get free somehow. Maybe Stanley could help them.

Michael pounded on the door and yelled, "Stanley, let go! Let go!"

"I don't believe this," said an Aldrich. "The vines are loosening. This plant is obeying a command. It's more valuable than we thought. We can up our price when we deliver it to our buyer."

He rapped on the door. "Thanks, kid. We wouldn't have known about this otherwise."

Michael whispered to Norman, "We have to get out of here." There was a sliver of light along the bottom of the door, so they could barely see each other. Norman began moving around.

"What are you doing?" whispered Michael.

"Looking for a light switch," said Norman. There was no switch on the wall, but he found a dangling string and pulled. A light bulb went on. They were surrounded by coats, winter boots, and neatly stacked storage boxes. Michael looked at the lock and hinges. Both had screws on the inside.

"Let's look in the boxes," he said. "Maybe we can find a screwdriver or something like that."

One box held a badminton set with rackets, the feathered shuttlecocks for batting back and forth, and a folded-up green net. In other boxes were neatly organized papers and clutter, but no screwdriver.

Michael slumped down on the floor, feeling totally discouraged.

"I wish I hadn't left my glue gun in the kitchen," said Norman.

"You put glue in your Blaster?" said Michael. "Cool."

"It's my invention," added Norman. "If I had it now, I could glue the door shut so they can't get us."

"Then we couldn't get out, either," Michael pointed out.

"Oh," said Norman. He thought a moment and suggested, "When they open the door, we can whack them in the knees with the badminton rackets. That might knock 'em over."

Michael replied, "We can try. If they ever open the door."

Norman said, "Aha! I just remembered something from my *How To Be a Detective* book." He put his eye to the keyhole. "With old locks like this that have long skinny keys, you can push the key out of the lock from the inside. But first you slide a sheet of paper under the door. The key falls on the paper. Then you pull it back under the door and unlock."

Michael said, "That might work. I think I saw somebody do it in a movie once." He took two pieces of paper from a box and folded one up into a narrow long shape to fit into the keyhole. They listened for a long time, trying to hear the twins' voices. They were going back and forth to the garage to load the van.

Once in awhile, the boys could make out what they were saying: "There isn't time to make two trips. We're just going to have to take the most valuable ones that'll fit into one van load and leave the rest."

"What are we going to do with those kids? We can't turn them loose."

The boys could not hear the answer.

When there had been silence for a few moments, Michael whispered, "Now."

Norman slid the paper under the door just below the lock. Michael poked into the keyhole. His spirits lifted as the key fell out. They heard it plop on the floor. They would be out of there in a moment, and out the front door in a flash. Norman carefully pulled the paper under the door. But the key was not on it.

Chapter 17

Norman lay his head sideways on the floor to try to see through the little space at the bottom so he could see where to aim the paper to slide it under the key. There was a rattle in the keyhole. The door opened.

"Were you looking for a key?" said one of the Aldriches. "Hey," he called to his brother. "They tried the old key-under-the-door trick. Remember we did that when we were kids? After we read about it in some book about how to be a detective?"

They heard his brother laughing in the other room. Norman reached into the badminton box to get a racket. Michael decided to try tackling the guy. That might keep him busy long enough to give Norman time to run out the front door and get help. But the man slammed the door and relocked it before they had a chance to do anything.

Michael squinted through the keyhole. He had a clear view of the opposite wall of the entryway. The key was gone.

"So much for the old key trick," said Michael. "But it almost worked."

Norman complained, "No fair! Why did they have to read a detective book, too?"

They sat clutching badminton rackets, ready to jump out swinging when they got another chance. Thunder rumbled. Another storm was starting. They put their ears against the door to try to hear what the Aldriches were doing.

"We've crammed as much as we can into the van," one said. "It's too bad we have to leave one of the big plants behind."

"Yeah, the buyer we've got lined up is willing to pay a lot. But at least we'll get a higher price for the one that obeys commands."

"I wish we didn't have to leave some of these other beauties behind, especially after all the trouble we went to get them. We'll have to leave the Chinese shrub, but the dozens of rain forest orchids will get us a thousand dollars apiece."

Norman whispered, "Did you hear that? They stole that bush! We can get the reward."

"First we have to get out of here," Michael said. "Be quiet so we can hear them."

One of the Aldriches was saying, "If those nosy kids hadn't barged in, we would have had time to make two trips tonight and take everything as planned. Come on. Their parents get home about six on Wednesdays. The sooner we get going, the longer the head start we'll have."

The other brother suggested, "If somebody rings the front doorbell, they might be able to hear the boys if they're yelling because the closet is so close by. Let's put them somewhere where it won't be so easy to hear them. That'll give us more hours to get farther away."

Suddenly the closet door opened. While one Aldrich blocked Michael, the other dragged out Norman, who kicked and tried to whack him with his racket. Michael was shoved to the back of the closet. The door was locked again. He pounded on it.

"You better not hurt my brother!" he yelled. "The police know all about you!"

"He's bluffing," one Aldrich said. "Hurry."

Michael was frantic. Were they taking Norman away in the van, too? He tried to calm down so he could think straight. But they had said there was no more room in the van. They had to be hiding Norman somewhere in the house. Michael wondered how he was ever going to get loose to rescue Norman and call the police to stop the crooks and bring Stanley back.

The Aldriches must have tiptoed because he did not hear them coming. They grabbed him out of the closet. One held him, although he squirmed and kicked. The other tied his feet together and his hands behind his back and hoisted him over his shoulder.

Down into the basement they went. The lights were on. At the bottom of the stairs sat Norman, who was tied the same way. He looked scared but glad to see Michael.

"Don't worry," said the Aldrich who sat Michael down on the cold floor. "You'll probably be able to wiggle out of these ropes in a few hours. Or someone will find you in a day or two." He took from his pocket the two breakfast bars that he agreed he would buy earlier. "If you get hungry, here's your band candy. If you get thirsty, use the water faucet in the laundry sink. Maybe you can turn it on with your nose and stick your mouth under it. Don't bother trying the old key trick. I'm taking the key." He laughed as he went up the stairs.

They heard the key turn and heavy footsteps hurrying on the floor above. The far-off sound of the van motor came from the attached garage. It moved away.

The house was silent, except for the sound of heavy rain outside. There was a boom of thunder.

"They're gone," said Michael. "And they said they were taking Stanley. Maybe they took Mrs. Smith's violet, too. We have to get loose before they get too far away."

Norman said, "Fluffy can help us. If he can get to a kitchen window, he can signal to Mom and Dad when they come home."

"We can't count on that," said Michael. "Start wiggling!" They both tried pulling their ankles and wrists apart to loosen the ropes but soon realized that it wasn't going to work.

Michael suggested, "If we put our backs to each other, maybe we can untie each other's hands."

They bumped and scrunched across the floor until they sat back to back. They were so eager to get untied that they both started at once and got their fingers in each other's way.

"Wait," said Michael. "I'll do yours first." He felt around to find the knot of the rope holding Norman's wrists and started trying to pick it apart. After a long time, he felt that it had loosened a little.

"How soon do you think Mom and Dad will get home?" asked Norman.

"I have no idea what time it is," replied Michael. "Move around to where I can see your watch." He saw that it was five o'clock. "We've got an hour. When we get untied we can climb up and open a window on the side of the basement next to our driveway. If we can't crawl out, at least we can yell to them when they get out of the car."

They both felt calmer now that they had a good plan. Michael kept working on Norman's knot. His fingers felt cramped, but he was determined to succeed.

Finally the knot came loose.

"There!" exclaimed Michael. "Now untie mine."

Norman struggled with the rope. "But mine's still tied," he said.

"I untied it," said Michael. "Move around and let me see." The knot was untied, but when Michael looked closely, he saw three more separate knots.

When he told Norman the bad news, Norman looked at Michael's wrists, hoping he was tied with only one. But there were four.

"Oh no," said Norman. They sat quietly for

a few moments, listening to the pouring rain. Near them in the basement, a quiet motor started up.

"It must be the pump that keeps water out of the basement," said Michael.

Norman said, "I better yell to Fluffy to let him know where we are. We heard the crooks walking around upstairs, so maybe he can hear us yell."

He began shouting, "Fluffy! Fluffy!"

Michael said, "He's not going to yell back."

"But he's got Margo's hamburger," explained Norman. "That's how I found him in the kitchen before. Be quiet and listen." He yelled the plant's name again.

Over the sound of the rain, they heard a faint *squeak!*

"Fluffy!" shouted Norman.

Squeak! Fluffy replied.

Michael said, "Wait a minute. That doesn't sound like it's coming from upstairs. It sounds closer. Call him again."

"Fluffy! Fluffy!"

Squeak! Squeak!

Michael turned his head to look at a far dark corner of the basement.

"It's coming from over there," he said.

Norman lay down, rolled over and over to the

stairs and pushed himself up to sit on the bottom one. Then he struggled up to sit on the next step, and the next. Swinging his legs over the side, he was able to stand up.

"Great master plan!" said Michael. He began rolling across the floor to the stairs so he could stand up, too.

Although Norman couldn't walk with his ankles tied together, he used tiny hops and shuffles to move slowly toward the dark corner. He almost tipped over a few times but kept going. When he got close, he found a door. He turned his back and got his hands around the knob. Fortunately, the door wasn't locked. It opened on his first try. Fluffy threw several vines out and wrapped them around Norman.

Norman told his plant why he couldn't hug back right now and said, "Hang on!" Shuffling and hopping, he towed Fluffy out of the little storage room and across the floor to the lighted area.

They decided to look for anything they could try to get Fluffy to use to cut their ropes but couldn't find scissors, knives, or anything else sharp. Fluffy accidentally knocked over a big plastic bottle of laundry detergent sitting on the dryer. The top had not been screwed on, so the blue liquid poured over the edge onto the floor.

"Be careful," Norman warned Michael. "Don't hop in it." The bottle continued to drool a widening pool. Michael thought, at least it wasn't the evil ooze. He wondered what Kevin would do in a situation like this. He knew they had to be ready to let Mom and Dad know where they were the minute the car pulled in, or they would miss their chance.

He looked up at the curtained high windows at ground level on that side of the basement.

He told Norman, "Some of Fluffy's vines could reach those windows. Can you get him to open one?"

Norman told Fluffy to reach for the curtains. Somehow the plant got the idea. He grabbed the rod holding the curtains and yanked it right off the window.

They saw it was not completely dark out, but still pouring rain. The window was locked. Neither the boys nor Fluffy would be able to open it.

"Now Mom and Dad can look in and see us," said Norman.

"If they look this way," said Michael. "We have to do something to get their attention. With the window closed, they won't hear us yelling."

Fluffy tapped a vine on the glass. It was a very soft sound.

"They'll never hear that," said Michael. "Not

in a rainstorm. If he banged the glass with something, that would work." They started looking for something Fluffy could bang with.

Then the overhead light went out, plunging them into darkness.

"Oh, no," exclaimed Norman. "The bulb burned out! Dad and Mom can't see us now when they look in."

Michael said, "I think the power's off. The pump just stopped, too."

Meanwhile, in their van full of plants, the Aldriches were driving very slowly because it was raining so hard they could barely see where they were going.

"Some getaway!" said Brett. "We could travel faster on tricycles."

"Quit complaining," replied Fred. "It's not safe to drive any faster in this storm. Let's pull off the road and wait till it lets up."

"No, we've got to get at least a couple of hundred miles away before we stop—even if we have to drive all night."

Fred said, "We could have gotten away last night without any problems if you hadn't wanted to make a try for those big plants."

"I would have got them," said Brett, "if I'd been right about nobody being home."

"You should have looked in the windows first."

"I did, but the curtains were all closed. I was sure they all went away in the car. Nobody answered when I called to double-check. And I'd made friends with the dog so it wouldn't bark. That came in handy this afternoon."

Fred kept changing radio stations, trying to find a weather report.

Brett said, "What was that? Did you hear a thump in the back?"

Fred turned around to look at their load of plants.

"Everything looks okay," he said.

"What about the big one that got its vines tangled around you?"

"It's right where I put it. Wrapping it in the badminton net we found in the closet was a good idea. I've never seen a plant with such wild vines." He added, "Better turn on the heat so the topical plants don't get chilled."

In the back, Stanley had quietly—except for the thump—succeeded in squeezing one vine out from under the net. He was working on another one.

Chapter 18

Back in the basement, Michael and Norman had decided that the only way to get the window open was to break it. Now that their eyes were used to the dark, they could see each other and Fluffy as dark shadows.

Because the plant was good at following certain directions he had been trained for, Norman kept calling, "Fluffy, grab! Fluffy, toss!"

Fluffy was pulling things off the many basement shelves and throwing them toward the window. When he threw the empty detergent bottle, it bounced off. A metal pail hit the wall with a clank. Norman urged Fluffy on. The plant kept up the target practice with food cans and small tools. Finally, with a quart can of paint, Fluffy hit the bullseye. Crash went the window.

Norman said, "Do you think we'll have to pay for fixing the window out of our allowances?"

"If we do," said Michael, "it'll be worth it."

On the highway, the rain had let up a little. Brett was driving faster now, almost up to the speed limit.

"We should make a quick stop to change license plates," he said. "It's unlikely that anyone in the neighborhood remembers our plate number, but just in case."

From the glove compartment, Fred took a set of license plates and a screwdriver.

"You'll have to hold the umbrella," he told Brett. "I don't want to get soaked."

When they saw a sign for a rest area coming up, they turned off. The area was deserted, which was just what they wanted.

Brett moved the gear shift to "Park," leaving the motor running to keep the heat on for the plants. Fred opened the umbrella and ran around to the driver's side. Together they splashed through puddles to the back of the van.

Inside, a vine crept over the back of the driver's seat. Then another vine, and another. After much tugging and twisting, Stanley had freed himself from the net.

The plant started grabbing at everything on the dashboard, exploring this strange place. He fiddled with the windshield wiper knob and changed the radio station. Holding the steering wheel, he dragged himself almost upright against the back of the seat.

Outside, Fred had taken the back plate off and lifted the other one to put on.

"That's strange," he said. "It sounds like the windows are going up and down."

"Just hurry up and put the plate on," snapped Brett. "My feet are getting soaked."

Stanley was playing with the automatic window controls. He also hit the switch that locked all the doors at once.

Brett and Fred were startled by headlights coming up toward them from the highway. It was a highway patrol car. Fred shoved all the license plates under his shirt and pressed his arm against them to hold them there. The car pulled up next to them. The officer was talking on his radio. Then he got out.

"Having a problem?" he said.

"No," said Brett. "We just pulled off the road to wait for the rain to let up."

"Drop the screwdriver," the officer ordered. Fred did.

"Whose van is this?" he asked.

"Mine," said Brett.

"Where's your license plate?"

"It was loose. We got out to fix it, but it must have fallen off."

The officer said, "I'll have to see your identification and van registration."

Fred and Brett pulled out their wallets and showed him licenses with fake names and addresses.

"Wait here," said the officer. He got into his car and radioed their names in for a check.

Brett whispered to Fred, "Don't worry. Those kids couldn't possibly have gotten loose and called the police so soon. It'll be quite a while before they start looking for twins in a brown van. By then we'll have changed vans."

The officer returned and said, "I'm giving you a ticket for not having a license plate."

Inside the van, Stanley was poking at the gear shift. He yanked hard, moving it from "Park" a couple of spaces over to "Drive." As many cars will do when put into gear, even without a foot on the accelerator, the van began moving slowly.

As it rolled away, Brett ran to the driver's

door to get in and stop it. He yanked on the handle. The door was locked. Fred ran to the passenger door. It was locked, too. They trotted along, keeping up with the van. It rolled a little faster.

Brett shouted, "Use your keys!"

Fred called back, "They're in my coat in the van."

They stopped running and watched helplessly as the van ran in circles around the rest area parking lot.

The officer radioed a call for help before he caught up with them. "So there's nobody in the van," he said. "And it's your van but you don't have the keys to unlock it. And you weren't going to use that screwdriver to break into it."

"Look out!" yelled Fred. They all jumped aside as the van rumbled by and headed for the rest rooms building. Narrowly missing that by turning left at the last minute, the van scraped a couple of picnic tables.

The officer said, "Whoever's at the wheel sure never passed the driver's license test."

The van bumped into a heavy rail fence and stopped. The officer ran over and shouted, "Come out of there slowly with your hands up!"

The window went down. Out came a couple of vines, held high.

Meanwhile, Michael, Norman, and Fluffy were leaning against the basement wall right under the broken window. The boys had no idea what time it was, so they were ready to start yelling the minute they heard the car.

"I'm tired," said Norman. "I can yell sitting down." He slid down with his back against the wall and plopped into an unexpected puddle.

"Oh, yuck!" he exclaimed. "The floor's all wet."

Michael hopped a couple of times and heard water. "The basement must be flooding because the pump stopped," he said.

"We're not going to drown, are we?" wailed Norman.

"No, it won't get that high."

"Are you sure?"

"Pretty sure. Besides, even if it did get that high, we can both swim."

"Not with our hands and feet tied," Norman pointed out.

Michael sighed. "We can both do the dead man's float," he reminded his brother. He felt water seeping into his shoes. It was getting higher.

"Don't say dead man," said Norman.

Michael said, "We can hop to the stairs and

stay above the water there, even if it gets really high. Which it's not going to."

"I can't hop," said Norman. "I'm sitting down and I can't get up without the stairs."

"You can roll over to them," said Michael.

"I don't want to," said Norman. "That'll get me all wet."

"If the water gets high, you'll get all wet anyway. But we have to stay by the window here, so Dad and Mom can hear us yell."

Norman said, "I can feel it getting higher." He wiggled his fingers. "It feels slippery," he said. "Sort of soapy."

"That must be the detergent mixing in the water," said Michael. "The basement is turning into a giant washing machine," he joked. "At least our sneakers will get clean."

Norman did not laugh.

"Don't worry," Michael told him. "Mom and Dad will be here soon."

They waited for what seemed like a really long time. The water crept higher and higher. It was halfway up to Michael's knees and getting close to Norman's shoulders.

Finally, they heard a car coming into the drive by the window.

"Mom! Dad! Help! Help!" they yelled. They

stopped to listen for an answer. The car motor was still going.

Michael said, "They haven't got out of the car yet. Keep yelling."

When Mom opened the door on the passenger side of the car near the basement window, their voices were drowned out by a long boom of thunder. At the same time Fluffy squeaked the hamburger, threw it out the window, reached a top vine out, and grabbed Mom's ankle.

As the sound of thunder died away, the boys heard a bloodcurdling scream.

"Hey, Mom!" yelled Michael. "Are we glad you're home!"

Chapter 19

After Mom and Dad figured out what was happening, Dad kept talking to the boys through the window while Mom called the police. The police came quickly. When they broke into the house in the dark, they tripped over a pair of large sneakers mysteriously stuck to the floor inside the front door. The boys heard them break open the basement door and saw their flashlights. Mom and Dad were right behind them, sloshing through the flood.

Officer Tim and Dad carried the dripping boys to the stairs and cut the ropes. Norman insisted some officers go back down and carry up Fluffy.

The boys told about the twins, the stolen plants, and the brown van. Norman added,

"The Chinese shrub is here, too. Can we have the reward?"

"We'll deal with the shrub later," said Officer Tim. "Right now we have to get out an all-points bulletin on the van. Too bad we don't have a license number. There are lots of brown vans."

"Aha!" exclaimed Norman. "I wrote down the license number. It's over at my house."

"Let's go get it," said Officer Tim. "You're a good little detective!"

Norman beamed with pride.

Michael poked him in the ribs with an elbow. "Not bad," he told Norman with a grin.

At the rest area, another patrol car had arrived. The first officer had found the two sets of license plates. He had run the numbers on his car computer for an identification, and was waiting for a reply.

A little later, at home in the kitchen, Michael and Norman were wolfing down sandwiches and milk when Officer Tim came by. The twins had been arrested, and the van full of plants was being brought back to town.

"Did you bring the reward?" Norman asked eagerly.

Officer Tim shook his head. "We searched the house, but the shrub's not there. We have a picture of its type of leaves photocopied from a botany book, so we'd know it if we saw it."

Michael said, "Then they changed their minds about leaving it behind, and it's in the van."

"I had an officer check," said Officer Tim. "It's not there either."

"It disappeared?" said Norman, looking baffled.

Michael thought there must be a logical explanation, but he had no idea what it might be. He decided to try to think like Sherlock Holmes. Maybe he could solve the mystery before Norman started babbling about helicopters and pterodactyls. But what popped into his mind was the Pat Jenkins method: If I were a shrub, where would I be? The only answer he could think of was: in a yard. But there were no shrubs in the Wards' yard—except—

"That's it!" he yelled.

"What's it?" asked Officer Tim.

Michael explained excitedly, "Maybe it's like the purloined letter. Nobody would notice a shrub that was planted in plain sight with other bushes. There's a bunch of them behind the Wards' garage."

Officer Tim led the way with his flashlight. He inspected the bushes and found that one's leaves were different from the others. He took the leaf picture from his pocket to check.

"This is it," he said.

"Yes!" shouted Norman. Michael beamed.

"Good work," said Officer Tim, patting Michael on the shoulder.

Stanley was home by nine-thirty. He looked very droopy from being squashed in a net and needing to be watered. Officer Tim said Michael could come to the police station tomorrow to identify Mrs. Smith's violet and take it home then.

"What's going to happen to the rest of the plants?" asked Michael.

"They'll be sent to plant rescue centers. Those are organizations that have greenhouse space and can care for them properly. The ones stolen in this country will be returned to where they came from if possible. And some countries want their stolen plants sent back. Any that can't be returned will be given to zoos or botanical gardens. Don't worry. They'll be well taken care of.

"And by the way, those twins had two sets of license plates and driver's licenses with six different last names. And they're wanted in Arizona for stealing saguaro cactuses from desert areas."

"What're those?" asked Norman.

"I know," said Michael. "They're the giant ones that look like they're holding up their arms bent at the elbows."

"Right," said Officer Tim. "You know a lot about plants." He told Dad and Mom, "You must be proud of these two. One's a plant expert, and they're both budding detectives."

Norman boasted, "I'm a plant expert, too."

"Good for you," said Officer Tim. "You're both outstanding young men. And you'll get the reward in a day or two."

Norman asked him, "Got any more cases you want help on?"

"Not right now," said Officer Tim.

"Thank goodness," said Mom.

After Stanley was watered and rolled back to his usual place in the boys' room, he perked up. Norman thought Fluffy looked tired from all the throwing he had done in the basement. They put out the plants' socks meals and got ready for bed. Margo curled up on the bottom of Michael's bed.

Michael decided to treat Stanley to a read-aloud bedtime story. He opened *The Revenge of the Werewolf Piano Teacher* and began: "As I sat down next to my teacher on the piano bench, I noticed that her hands looked hairier than usual. Or was I imagining that?

"Her fingers rippled over the keys. The music began to sound weird.

" 'Tonight the moon will be full,' she growled. Had her voice sounded that way before? Was that a moustache starting to grow on her upper lip?

" 'On a night like this,' she snarled, 'I feel angry if students haven't practiced their lessons. Did you practice?'

"I had not, so I tried to change the subject. 'What great teeth you have,' I said politely.

"There was a loud scratching at the door. Suddenly . . ."

Suddenly Norman slid out of bed. He grabbed his flutophone and ran out of the room. Soon from the bathroom came the eerie notes of Norman playing musical scales.

Mom came down the hall. She looked in and asked Michael, "Why is he playing at this time of night?"

Michael replied, "With everything that went on today, I guess he forgot to practice." Mom went back to the living room. The flutophone notes wailed on. Stanley pulled himself to the door, closed it, and came back beside Michael. He tapped the book with a vine.

Michael started reading where he left off: "Suddenly, someone—or something—outside the door began to howl."